THE FUNDAMENTAL TRUTH

BY

I. A. SHEPHERD

I. A. SHEPHERD

Copyright © 2018 I.A.SHEPHERD

All rights reserved.

ISBN-13: 978-1-9808-3923-1

CONTENTS

	Prologue	7
1	ARBROATH SCOTLAND, JULY 1950	14
2	AUGUSTA GEORGIA APRIL 1953	17
3	ARBROATH SCOTLAND JULY 1953	26
4	FORT WORTH TEXAS NOVEMBER 1953	41
5	ARBROATH JULY 1968	44
6	AUGUSTA GEORGIA NOVEMBER 1968	59
7	AUGUSTA GEORGIA APRIL 1972	64
8	ARBROATH JULY 1975	67
9	AUGUSTA GEORGIA APRIL 1986	76
10	ARBROATH JULY 1999	77
11	AUGUSTA GEORGIA APRIL 2007	96
12	ARBROATH JULY 2007	101
13	NEW YORK AUGUST 2008	113
14	AUGUSTA GEORGIA APRIL 2017	117
15	ROYAL BIRKDALE ENGLAND JULY 2017	127
16	AUGUSTA GEORGIA APRIL 2018	137
17	ARBROATH JULY 2018	141
18	AUGUSTA GEORGIA DECEMBER 2024	157
19	AUGUSTA GEORGIA 2034	166
20	ARBROATH JULY 2034	176

I. A. SHEPHERD

21	AUGUSTA GEORGIA APRIL 2051	189
22	ARBROATH JULY 2051	201
23	AUGUSTA GEORGIA APRIL 2062	214
24	ARBROATH JULY 2062	220
25	AUGUSTA GEORGIA APRIL 2070	223
26	MOON WORLD NOVEMBER 2072	227
27	AUGUSTA GEORGIA APRIL 2073	231
28	ANTARTICA MAY 2073	236
29	CARNOUSTIE JUNE 2073	239
30	MFF MOONBASE OCTOBER 2073	240
31	AUGUSTA GEORGIA APRIL 2086	244
32	AUGUSTA GEORGIA APRIL 2091	250

About The Author

ACKNOWLEDGEMENTS

I would like to thank my two daughters for their help with this book. To Karen for all her hard work in getting this book to print and to Elaine for her artwork on the cover.

Thanks also to my wife, Glenda for her support in this new venture.

Disclaimer

This is a work of fiction. Names, characters, places and incidents are either the product of the author's imagination or are used fictitiously and any resemblance to actual persons, living or dead, business establishments, events or locations are entirely coincidental.

PROLOGUE

Normandy June 6th 1944

Supreme commander of the allied forces, Dwight David Eisenhower surveyed the scene before him. He could hardly see water, such was the density of the fleet. He was nervous.

He had taken to the game of golf some 10 years earlier and was thinking back to a time he was in the company of his friend Bobby Jones, who was in the process of creating a golf course in Augusta Georgia, where he could invite his friends for some springtime fun and competition.

"The golf course chooses its champion," said Bobby, "all you can do is work out your strategy. Stay calm, think clearly, and see how the cards fall."

Dwight, who enjoyed a game of poker, knew the sense in this, he knew that the strategy he had engaged in today was probably the biggest gamble he would ever make. The bluff was on, thousands of lives depended on it. He hoped and prayed his gamble would succeed.

****

Peter Shepherd, Tom Beattie and Alec Cargill had joined the Black-watch after the outbreak of the war against Germany.

They'd seen action all over the various theatres of conflict.

As fishermen from the east coast of Scotland, their jobs were seen as essential to support the war effort.

The town of Arbroath was well served by fishermen, many of whom, recently retired, were able to convince the authorities that they could return to the sea, and release the young men of the town to help the war effort by joining the armed forces.

They were expecting carnage as they sat in the landing craft approaching the beach. The weather was anything but gentle.

"Reminds me of the run in to the harbour in a south easterly," laughed Alec who was the sergeant in charge. He had a way with words that inspired his men and lightened their mood.

As the dancing craft approached, the three friends were unaffected by the motion, unlike some of their land based comrades. When the ramp descended, there was little time to think as they scrambled ashore. Surprisingly, there was no gunfire to meet them.

Earlier that day, British Commandos had stormed the German strongholds, completing a successful and essential manoeuvre. When they got to the top of the beach, a bit wet, but otherwise unscathed, they were able to lie down and take stock.

"Ok men," shouted Alec, "keep your eyes peeled, there could be a few stray Germans hidden away."

As the afternoon stretched on and command got

organised, some semblance of order surrounded the scene.

"That wasn't so bad," said Peter "I expected a lot worse."

"You always do," laughed Tom. "Pete the pessimist permanently gloomy," he sang, "always moaning, always doomy, the end is nigh he's prone to sigh, should've been a minister and that's no lie."

The group chuckled; they'd heard that one before. In the distance, they could hear the unmistakable symphony of modern warfare. They knew where they were headed and they knew the Germans were waiting.

They crossed the River Orne and headed east.

"A bit different from North Africa," piped up Peter.

"Stating the obvious," said Alec.

"It's not a desert," laughed Tom adding, "and there'll be no oasis to relax and put your feet up."

"I've read though, that this part of France is famous for its dairy produce, so in my view, an oasis is what it is" said Peter.

"Well I hope we get the chance to hang around and sample the cheese," said Alec.

"And the wine," said Tom, "I've never tasted wine."

"No?" inquired Alec, "What about that single malt that your partial to, you know, wine of the Spey Valley region."

"That's not wine, that's whisky," replied Tom.

"Non monsieur," said Alec. "Water ingested, nicely enhanced. The term can be applied to all water based liquids, which have been created for human consumption and improved by the addition of alcohol."

Tom laughed. "So I suppose for you Sarge, the wine of choice is McEwans Export."

"Only on a Saturday night, accompanied by a game of darts of course" said Alec.

"The perfect partner," said Peter. "I of course prefer a half and a half on a Saturday night, gets me in the mood for the dancing at the Marine."

"You mean the swaying on the pavement," laughed Alec. "Your attendance at the Marine has been recorded at only 4 visits over the last year, not very a good return given some 20 attempts."

"Most of those attempts never left the pub" protested Peter, "due to a series of domino matches with my grandad."

"Aye, they certainly had the domino effect on you," stated Alec, "you've got to choose, dominos or dancing. I can tell you, Glenda prefers dancing."

"Ok," said Peter when we get back I'll give Grandad the bad news."

That night they slept in a barn just a mile north of Reviers, having seen nothing of the enemy that first day.

The next morning they awoke to the sound of artillery bombardment to the south west.

THE FUNDAMENTAL TRUTH

"Sounds about 10 miles away," ventured Peter.

"Aye, and I've a feeling were going to be a lot closer before the day's out," said Alec.

By mid-morning they were on the move. Early June in Normandy, the colours and smells were a delight on the senses.

"Lovely part of the world," said Tom as they marched along one of the many lanes that criss-crossed the landscape. "Reminds me of the Strathmore Valley, without the mountains of course."

"Don't see many berry fields," said Alec, "plenty of apples though," as he picked some off an overhanging tree. After passing them round, he reminded all who could hear him.

"Remember men these beautiful fruits remind us of why we are here. To get rid of the Nazis who would turn this world grey and dark, savour this fruit and remember the taste when you come face to face with the enemy."

Light was failing and the CO came back along the lines to thank the troops for their efforts and that they had reached their objective for day 2. Camp would be made along a small river where the men could wash and relax.

The next day was a different matter. The troops had been ordered to attack a radar station at Douvres, where they encountered the infamous SS 12th Panzer Division.

The land around them exploded, as shell after shell pounded their position. The C.O. Colonel Thomson ordered a retreat.

"That was a bit noisy," said Alec as the retreat got underway, "I thought radar stations were supposed to be quiet places."

"They are," said Tom, "the gentle sweep of the radar picking up the odd blip of ships and planes as they go on their merry way."

"Where are we headed now Sarge?" asked Peter.

Alec smiled, "I hear we're headed south to support the 6th Airbourne division, they're struggling to hold some bridge that the General's think is very important to the breakout."

Pegasus Bridge as it would come to be known, crossed the Caen Canal and had been captured in the early hours of June 6th. It had been primed for demolition by the defenders if there was a risk that it could be captured.

Tom decided that a song was in order now that they had survived their first skirmish. "Where hae ye been sae braw lad...?" he started, the rest joined in, knowing the words to the "Bard's" song intimately.

It felt good. They somehow knew, however, that where they were headed, the Devil would be waiting.

The news got back to Arbroath of the men's fate. Three little boys watched their Mums and grannies cry. They would hear many tales of their Dads' bravery, how they tried to save each other, how they fought and fought against the odds, how they never gave up, even at the end.

How they roared, until their last breath they roared, and then they were silent. They would remember them.

THE FUNDAMENTAL TRUTH

I. A. SHEPHERD

1

ARBROATH SCOTLAND JULY 1950

Professional golfer Jack Stewart was in his workshop, re-gripping a few clubs for the local golf club members. Typical of golf in Scotland at the time, Golf Clubs were attached to public links courses, which were situated on land owned by the local councils.

The James Braid designed links course, was very popular with the residents of the town and Jack was kept busy in his small wooden shop beside the first tee. He heard the door of the front shop creak open and knew he had a customer.

It was the first Saturday in July which meant that the Arbroath open amateur tournament was the competition of the day.

"Hello Jack," said the voice belonging to Alec Shepherd, a local fisherman and a keen weekend golfer.

"Hello Alec," replied Jack, "long-time no see, what have you been up to?"

"Long story" said Alec," a fishy one involving a lot of salmon. The drift-netting's been very productive lately so I've had no time for golfing, or anything else for that matter."

"You playing today? I don't see your name down."

"No Jack, not today. I'm too tired. I just came out for

a blether."

"Sit down man," said Jack. "I'll just put the kettle on."

Once the tea was made, they sat down facing each other across the workshop table.

"I've been keen to talk to you about the US Open at Merion," said Alec.

"I know," said Jack, "I've been thinking about little else since." His expression turned grim.

"You know Alec when Ben Hogan's car was hit by that bus last year the whole sporting world knew about it. We were shocked when we saw photos of the wreckage, amazed that anyone could survive such an impact." He took a sip of his tea then continued.

"It was touch and go for quite a while; it took tremendous skill to keep him alive. I remember the Airforce sent a plane down to New Orleans to pick up a specialist surgeon to work on him."

"I remember that," said Alec "people thought he'd never walk again let alone play golf. He's made of tough oak Jack, I think losing his father when he was a young boy flicked a switch in him, drew him into himself, created an impenetrable shell which helped him become a very focused individual." He smiled in admiration.

"That situation when he threw himself across his wife's lap was a demonstration of the freedom to act instinctively and selflessly, which I think was created by the loss of his father."

"How very observant of you," laughed Jack, "didn't

know you were a psychiatrist?"

"I'm not as you well know," laughed Alec, "but the losses suffered due to the war created many real life situations in Arbroath, I see similarities. I kind of look after my nephew Gary who lost his Dad in '44. He was only 2 then but he's very aware now of what happened. The sacrifice, the hero, it's inspiring to him."

"Do you think Hogan will continue to inspire?" asked Jack. "Those injuries will take their toll over time. He's now in his forties after all."

"No doubt about it," replied Alec, "he's a very driven individual. I just hope one day he comes over here."

"There's talk of the Open coming to Carnoustie in '53," said Jack.

"Hogan's never played in it," said Alec.

"I know," said Jack, "I think you're going to have to catch a lot more salmon Alec, a trip across the pond will be required if you want to see him live."

They both laughed.

2

AUGUSTA   GEORGIA   APRIL 1953

Ben Hogan and Jimmy Demaret were practising together, preparing for the start of the annual Masters Invitational Golf Tournament, held every April, at the golf course created by Bobby Jones.

After he retired from competitive golf in 1930, Bobby wanted to build a golf course near his home, where he could invite his many friends for some southern hospitality, with the occasional, "birdie" thrown in.

The first tournament, held in 1934, was won by an American named Horton Smith. His great putting skills served him well on Augusta's undulating surfaces. The publicity surrounding the first tournament was pretty low key and the golfing public at large quickly forgot the result.

April generally was a quiet time for American sports. The football season was over and the summer long baseball season was just getting under way.

It was the following year, however, that the tournament really hit the headlines.

Friends and rivals Gene, "The Squire" Sarazen and Walter "The Haig" Hagen were on the 14th hole of the 4th and final round when they heard a roar that could only mean a birdie was secured by the leader on the final hole.

It looked to the Haig that the tournament was out of their reach, and he indicated as much to the Squire.

"That's not like you," said Gene, "to give up that easily, we've still got 5 holes to go, who knows, the ball can go in from anywhere."

"Ok," laughed Hogan, "let's have a go, I love a gamble."

The pair of them lost their inhibitions and attacked on every shot coming in. The very next hole, the Squire had 235 yards to carry the water hazard in front of the green.

Tournament host Bobby Jones was among 12 spectators to the side of the green. He sensed something interesting was about to happen.

Sure enough, the Squire selected a 4-wood and hit the most beautiful draw. As it turned from right to left it looked like it wouldn't quite make the carry. As it came down, the patron's held their breath and the ball landed on the steep slope in front of the green, bounced high enough to just make the surface, and began to roll slowly but unerringly like a putt towards the hole, and in.

Bobby smiled and clapped knowing that history was unfolding before him. His golf course had chosen its champion.

Ben and Jimmy were great friends from Texas, widely recognised as the foremost shot makers in the world of professional golf.

"So Jimmy," said Ben, "you've got 242 yards and I've got 239, the pin's middle of the green, what do you see?"

The Tuesday of Masters week was when the players could get their final full day's practice in as the par 3 competition was held on the Wednesday.

THE FUNDAMENTAL TRUTH

Jimmy knew what Ben was really asking.

"What's the bet, Ben?" He laughed, knowing that the Squire's legendary shot," heard around the World", was about to be attempted.

"The usual," said Ben, which meant a bottle of Speyside single malt whisky,"10 year old Glenlivet."

"What if I hole it?" laughed Jimmy.

"Then you'll be buying a dozen," said Ben, "drinks all round, anyway enough chat we're holding the group up behind."

"It's only Gene, he can wait," said Jimmy.

"New Yorkers are impatient Jimmy."

"He can't reach out here, he can swing away anytime."

"True," laughed Ben.

Jimmy D swung away with a 3-wood, staying back a little longer he knew a high draw would result. A majestic shot arced its way towards the green, landing front right and tracking on the slope to within 25 feet of the flag.

"Shot," said Ben who selected the same club and made his move. Ben had been developing a fade as his go-to shot under pressure and he was under pressure here.

The lie he had was slightly uphill and right to left, favouring the draw as demonstrated by Jimmy. Ben agreed with Jimmy on the shot selection, but his was a lower trajectory releasing up the green to rest 20ft behind the flag.

"Great shot my friend," said Jimmy.

"Thanks Jimmy," said Ben, "I learned that one from you."

"I know you did Ben, I taught you everything you know."

They both laughed as they headed into the evening sun.

Later in the clubhouse, Jimmy presented Ben with his prize which would be opened after the champion's dinner and shared among the past masters.

The dinner this year, only the second such occasion, was hosted by Sam Snead, the 1952 champion. Sam's dinner menu was traditional southern fare, which met with universal approval.

Tournament host Bobby Jones got up to speak. After thanking Sam for his excellent choice, and the staff for their presentation, tradition dictated that he recount his experience when he first set eyes on the property, where his dream became a reality.

"When Clifford and I came across this piece of land, I knew immediately that this was the place. The contours, the water, the colours, my senses were in overdrive.

There was something more though, a presence....It's difficult for me to describe the sensations we were experiencing as Clifford and I walked the property."

He smiled, "As the warm breeze made the bushes shimmer it was like music, like an Orchestra playing a beautiful symphony. The planet was singing and we were its captive audience."

"Golf gentlemen, at it's very best, played by the very best, enhances the symphony. You, the conductors, wave your batons and launch poetry into the sky, the planet plays with your prose, adjusts it as the mood takes her, and leaves you to accept the result.

"A humbling experience indeed. You, the Masters, gentlemen have shown humility of the highest order. The golf course chooses its champion."

Applause and stamping of feet.

Each of the former champions in turn, stood and entertained the audience with tales of their own, which became more outrageous as the single malt flowed.

First 3-time winner Jimmy Demaret was the last to rise... and fall... and rise again.

"My names JD not JC," laughed green suede shoes clad Jimmy. "Hope you like my outfit." He gestured towards his aqua marine trousers, canary yellow shirt, and the Lone Star of Texas tie.

"I toned it down a bit for this formal occasion, normally when I go out to dinner I have to hand out sunglasses to the folks in the restaurant."

He continued. "Can I just say Bob, it's such a pleasure being back here at your lovely spread. When I say spread I don't mean a Texas spread full of cow shit, and horse manure, I mean a genteel type of spread, kinda like Rhett Butler's place in Gone with the Wind."

Murmurs of agreement.

"As the first 3-time winner I have to take issue with your description of and I quote: 'A beautiful symphony the planet was singing'."

"I have to tell you when I hear the bushes shimmering, panic sets in as it reminds me of my childhood when I fell into poison ivy.

I knew the pain was only gonna get worse, Augusta has that effect on you."

Laughter.

"Suffer for your pleasure, no pain no gain. I get so nervous on the first tee I have to sing to myself to get the ball on the tee."

He then began to sing: "Let's take it nice and easy, it's gonna be so easy, for us to fall in love, hey baby what's your hurry, relax and don't you worry, we're gonna fall in love, we're on the road to romance, that's safe to say, buts let's make all the stops, along the way, the problem now of course is, to simply hold your horses, to rush would be a crime, cause nice and easy does it every time"...

Cue much applause.

"Nice song Jimmy, haven't heard that one before" piped up Gene.

"I know Gene," said Jimmy, "that's 'cause I sing it to myself, no one can hear it but me." Chuckles.

"Effective though, stops me shaking."

THE FUNDAMENTAL TRUTH

"Less booze would have the same effect" laughed Gene.

"True," said Jimmy who slumped back in his chair.

"Thanks Jimmy," said Bob, "the voice is as good as ever. Ok gentlemen those of you who can, please go through to the sitting room where the entertainment can continue, Jimmy here is just getting warmed up." And he was.

Next morning nursing a slightly sore head, Jimmy D headed down to the range where he knew he would find Ben. Hogan smiled as he saw his friend approach.

"Aah the phoenix rises... you have a good night Jimmy?"

"A good morning to you too" laughed Jimmy, "got to bed
3 hours ago came down to check on you, where'd you disappear to?"

You know me Jimmy 3 whiskies and I get very drowsy, must be the painkiller combo."

"Yeah that'll do it ...every time" laughed Jimmy.

"I've been thinking about my schedule for this year Jimmy, the pain is getting worse. The British Open is at Carnoustie this year which they say is the best and fairest test on their rota." Ben's expression was thoughtful.

"I'd like to play it at least once before my legs can't carry me. The PGA clashes with the British and being match-play, is potentially a lot more walking. Valerie of course, is not averse to the idea of a holiday across the pond."

"Great idea," said Jimmy, "I may come myself; I hear there are at least 50 single malts I haven't tried yet."

"No," said Ben, "you have tried 'em, you just don't remember." He chuckled at Jimmy's solemn expression.

"I don't think Bob's very pleased with me after last night's performance."

"How do you know?" enquired Ben.

"I saw my green jacket hanging on the outside of the locker room door."

"Oh dear," said Ben, "that's not good."

Five days later, the tournament was over.

"28 shots," Ben said, "that's 7 per round, how many whiskies did you drink Jimmy?"

"7 per round," laughed Jimmy, "that's glasses not bottles and it was after each round not during. I knew you had me after you shot 66 to my 80. So what's the damage?"

"$10 a shot," said Ben, "as if you didn't know."

"Cash or cheque," said Jimmy.

"You don't have that much cash," laughed Ben, "so I know it's a cheque."

"I'll get it framed for you," said Jimmy, "you can hang it on your locker door." He smiled. ,"Joking aside Ben, that was an awesome performance this week, 274 round

THE FUNDAMENTAL TRUTH

here is a record score, you must be very proud."

"To tell you the truth Jimmy, I feel very blessed. I felt the golf course was helping me out there all week. I could see each shot pretty clearly before I swung the club, I've never felt so calm or played so free, it was pure joy."

"Two jackets Ben, one to go, they say third one's always the toughest."

They both laughed.

3

ARBROATH SCOTLAND JULY 1953

The boys were excited, they knew of course of the coming of the Open Championship to Carnoustie. Their home town of Arbroath, just 7 miles up the coast was full of strange faces and unusual voices.

The "3 Amigos" also knew of the arrival at the open of the most famous golfer in the world, an American named Ben Hogan.

The newspapers and radio had been full of stories about the great man, how he had won this year's Masters Tournament at Augusta, Georgia, and the US Open at Oakmont, Pennsylvania.

The papers wrote about his amazing ability to hit fairway after fairway and green after green. Nobody, they said, had ever struck a golf ball with such precision or worked harder to achieve their goals.

The boys, however, whilst being impressed by his golfing achievements, were much more interested in a particular story about a car crash that occurred in 1949.

The story revealed that Ben had thrown his body across the seat of his car to protect his wife Valerie from the inevitable impact, head on, with a bus. This selfless act almost killed Ben and did in fact, save Valerie's life.

Ben was in hospital for many months, severely injured, with friends and family fearing he would never walk again, let alone play golf. Ben did walk again, and boy did he play golf.

The three friends talked about this, and what it meant to them.

Alec, Ian and Gary had all been born in 1943 in the fishing town of Arbroath. They had known their fathers only briefly before they were killed in action during the 1944 invasion of Normandy.

Now aged 10 respectively, they had been brought up by their Mums, grannies and aunties (their grandads and uncles being at sea most of the time) and became close friends, although not related. They became like a band of brothers.

Gary Shepherd was the youngest, although that fact didn't inhibit him when it came to giving an opinion on the important issues of the day, like the best spot to catch crabs when the tide was out. He loved his football and was always available for a kick around at Victoria Park.

Ian Beattie was a couple of months older than Gary and the extra experience certainly counted. Many a time wise words from Ian had saved the accident prone youngster from a visit to the infirmary. Ian loved the outdoor life and he swam like a dolphin. He was destined for a life at sea.

Alec Cargill was the oldest of the Arbroath Triumvirate and such was the leader. He was the studious one and spent almost every Saturday morning in the Library, at Hill Place. There he would discover the written word, where the many mysteries of the world and beyond, could be discovered.

I. A. SHEPHERD

The three amigos had been told of their father's bravery, and sacrifice each had made attempting to save the other. There was something about Ben Hogan that drew the boys to him. He had survived.

So it was agreed between the Mums, grannies and aunties, that the boys be allowed to go to Carnoustie for the day to watch the golf - at least that's what the boys told them.

It was decided that they accompany their Mums on the train to Dundee at 9.00am, be dropped off at Carnoustie, and picked up again at 5.00pm.

Their Mums would be busy selling the baskets of Smokies, Kippers etc.to the good people of Dundee.

It was a beautiful morning as they set off with their supply of food for the day, along with pencils and paper. Alec thought it important to make a record of their adventure, for study later.

When they got to Carnoustie, they were met with a sea of canvas, which they discovered was a tented village associated with the event.

Adults and children wandered about the village looking at the latest golfing equipment and clothing. There were tents for eating and drinking in and there was even a tent for the members of the press.

As this was a practice day, the crowds weren't too large and the boys were able to wander freely, amazed at the scene.

"Where's Ben Hogan?" asked Gary to no one in particular.

"Do you know what he looks like?" asked Ian.

"Only that he wears a white hat," replied Gary.

"That's a big help," said Ian.

"He's an American," stated Alec.

"What's that?" enquired Gary.

"That's where he lives," stated Alec, "In America."

"Same place as Roy Rogers?"

"Aye."

"We'll need to ask somebody if they've seen him," said Alec. The three then wandered off.

After a while, they came across a tent with a few golf bags outside with the sign, CADDIES above the door. Gary wandered in and was immediately choking; such was the density of the smoke inside.

A large ruddy faced man in tweeds turned to see Gary at the door and announced, "You can't come in here laddie."

Gary caught his breath enough to manage a "Have you seen Ben Hogan?"

"Aye laddie," came the reply, "I saw him about an hour ago as he came off the course. He's probably gone for some breakfast."

Gary reported back to the others waiting outside and

the talk of breakfast prompted an agreement that they sit down and eat.

They'd each been given an array of items to eat, sandwiches, apples, pork pies and a bottle of milk each. They'd all brought their school bags to manage the load. During their snack they discussed the next move.

"Where will he eat his breakfast?" asked Gary.

"Probably in one of those tents," said Ian, "or maybe that café across the road."

"We should try that first," said Alec. So they went.

"Have you seen Ben Hogan?" asked Gary of the waitress in the café.

"No son, I hear he's at the practising."

"Where's that?"

"On that big piece of grass beside the beach."

"Ok thanks."

The boys made their way back past the tents towards the beach and they came to a large expanse of grass. Here they could hear the sound of club-head meeting ball before a gathered audience.

They made their way into and through the crowd to the front. A number of players were swinging away, and the audience seemed mesmerised by the proceedings.

The boys ambled along the line stopping occasionally to watch the hitting of the balls. Ian was the first to break the silence.

"Do you see how far those balls are flying," said Ian.

"A lot further than you can kick a football," laughed Gary. "Which one's Ben Hogan?"

"He isn't here," said the tall man standing behind them.

"Will he be coming here after his breakfast?" asked Gary.

"How do you know he's at his breakfast?" asked the man.

"A big fat man in one of those tents told me."

"That'll be right enough then," smiled the man.

The boys had a chat and decided to wait a while and see if Ben Hogan would come after he finished his breakfast.

They were particularly impressed by a young Englishman, who, after whispering to neighbours, discovered his name to be Peter Allis.

The young professional was displaying a wonderful array of shots, high and low, left and right.

Alec couldn't resist. "Excuse me Mr Allis." Peter looked round and smiled when he saw the source of the voice. "Yes young man what can I do for you?"

"I was wondering if I could have a go, I've never played golf and you make it look so easy." "Why thank you young man, you're very kind, but I don't think the R&A

would be too pleased if we professionals invited young men like you onto the practice ground to hit balls."

"Ok," said Alec, "I understand. Do you know Ben Hogan?"

Peter was impressed by the quick change of tact and smiled. "I certainly do" he said, "why do you ask?"

"We're hoping to see him today, but we've never met him, what's he like?"

"He's a great man," said Peter, "and I'm not just talking about his ability to strike a golf ball, as great as that is. There's a presence about him, as if he knows something the rest of us don't."

Peter wondered for a moment why he had just said that and Alec filled the void.

"He survived." Peter looked at the 3 boys quizzically; he knew they meant the accident. "Good luck," he said, "I hope you find what you're looking for."

"Good luck to you too," said Alec, "I hope the golf course is kind to you."

They parted.

"That was great," enthused Gary. "We have to give that game a try."
"We will," said Alec, "maybe next week."

Meanwhile, there was no sign of Ben Hogan. As the tide was coming in, the boys decided to go down to the beach. They crossed the Barry Burn and headed west. The sand dunes got bigger and bigger the further they walked.

THE FUNDAMENTAL TRUTH

Eventually, they came to a fence with a red flag flying above, a man in uniform approached. "Sorry boys, the beach is closed beyond here, the Army's practising their shooting."

"Ok," they said and made their way back about 100 yards where the dunes were only 50ft high. After much jumping and rolling, they began to tire. They agreed that more food was required before any further activity could take place. So they ate.

Meanwhile, back in Arbroath, Ben's caddy Cecil Tims had suggested a morning trip to the fishing town for a seafood breakfast. Although Ben was happy to do this, he was well aware of Cecil's reputation of, see food and eat it.

The famous Arbroath Smokie was the delicacy on Cecil's mind, and when they arrived at a fish merchant on the High St. they could smell the process was well underway.

Matthew and Margaret Smith were well known in the town for producing fish products of the highest quality. Margaret's skills with a filleting knife were second to none.

Ben and Cecil wandered in and Matthew came out to greet them, reeking of wood smoke. Matthew, a keen weekend golfer himself recognised Hogan immediately.

"Fit like Ben," he announced shaking hands, "pleased to meet you." Ben smiled and thought immediately, this place was like Texas; the people were warm and looked you straight in the eye when they met you for the first time.

"My pleasure," said Ben, "Matthew is it?"

"Aye," said Matthew, "what can I do for you?"
"We'd like a pair of Smokies for our breakfast," said Ben. "Make that two pairs," piped up Cecil.

Matthew smiled, "They'll be ready in about 5 minutes. Have a seat. Would you like a cup of tea?" Nods of approval, so the kettle was put on.

"What do you think of the course at Carnoustie?" enquired Matthew.

"I think it's a pretty fair test of golf," said Ben, "most of the trouble is on the left, but the bunkering means you can't bail out right if the fear takes hold, suits my preferred fade shape of shot."

"Do you like playing in the wind?" asked Matthew.

"I sure do," said Ben, "back in Texas we get a lot of wind. It defines you as a ball striker. Using the small ball in the wind should help as it tends to fly a little lower."

Just then Gary's Mum Glenda came into the shop looking for some natural smoked haddock, essential ingredient for her famous fish soup.

"Morning Glenda," said Matthew. "Would you like a cup of tea? We're just having a break and a blether."

"I'd love one," said Glenda, "and I'd also like one of those hot Smokies I could smell from down the road."

"Just coming up," laughed Matthew. "Take a seat."

Ben and Cecil were introduced and the four sat down to enjoy breakfast.

THE FUNDAMENTAL TRUTH

The chat came easy between the four, many stories were exchanged, and when it came to parting, Ben told Glenda, "I'll keep a lookout for the boys."

On arriving back at Carnoustie, Ben and his caddy made their way to the first tee where they were due off at 12.30. The time was chosen 6 hours after they had teed off that morning.

Ben had anticipated, after looking at the weather forecast and tide charts, that there was a chance of a sea breeze that afternoon. Playing holes 1 to 9 again that day underlined the meticulous preparation typically undertaken by Hogan at a tournament.

Given that the 9th green was only half a mile from his practice facility at Barry, made the decision easy as he could walk there unnoticed. When Ben teed off there were little more than a dozen people milling around, he was happy.

Meanwhile, back at the dunes, the Three Amigos were lazing around enjoying the sunshine.

Looking back towards the town, Gary suggested they head back towards the practice area to check if Ben Hogan was there. Ian agreed.
"We need to find out what time it is, remember we need to be at the train station for 5 o'clock."

Alec, who was busy reading and adding to his notes, nodded. From their high vantage point looking down they could see the whole golf course stretching out before them.

"Isn't that Ben Hogan there?" enquired Alec. The second green was only 100 yards from where they stood and there was a golfer in a white hat strolling onto the green.

"He's walking with a limp," said Gary, "so it could be him."

The boys made their way over to the green. They thought they recognised him, from newspaper pictures. As Hogan walked up towards the third tee, Gary decided to confirm.

"Are you Ben Hogan?"

"Are you Gary Shepherd?"

"I am," said Gary.

"Well I'm Ben Hogan, pleased to meet you."

"Pleased to meet you too, how do you know my name?"

"I met your mom this morning in Arbroath; she told me all about you and your two buddies there."

The boys exchanged glances.

Hogan laughed. "Don't worry, it was all good."

"Can we watch you play golf?" asked Alec.

"Sure son, I take it you're Alec and this here is Ian?"

The boys nodded.

For the next two hours, the boys wandered the fairways alongside Ben, enthralled by the seeming ease, with which he despatched each shot towards the intended target.

As Hogan left the 9th green, he called over.
"So boys did you enjoy watching the golf?"

They all nodded. "How do you do it?" asked Alec who'd been making notes on his observations.

"Well Alec, I was just a little bit older than you guys, when I started and I learned by watching the good players in my home town and tried to copy them.

As I got older and stronger, I just loved the feeling of smacking that ball just as hard as I could so I could watch it fly."

"Do you think we could do that one day?" asked Alec.

"Sure you could, if you put your mind to it, you can do most anything you want."

The boys looked at each other, and back at Hogan who smiled and said.

"Don't worry boys, your journey's only just beginning, many roads to travel before you find your chosen path. Have fun"!

With that Hogan bade them farewell, adding that he hoped to see them again during the week ahead.

Gary turned to his pals and asked, "What did he mean; your journey's just beginning?"

"I think he's been speaking to your Mum," said Alec who understood that Hogan wasn't talking about golf.

"What did she tell him?"

"You'll have to ask her, but I think it was about your Dad."

Gary seemed a little confused.

"I don't think my Dad played golf."

"No he was a bowler," said Ian.

"How do you know that?"

"I've seen the old set of bowls in the back-house," said Ian.

"I thought they were weights for the fishing nets?" said Gary.

"No, weights for the fishing nets are made of lead, wood floats," laughed Ian.

"You've got lead for brains," said Alec. "Let's go."

They made their way back to the train station where Auntie Agnes would meet them and escort them back to Arbroath.

"Mum, we met Ben Hogan," said Gary.

"So did me," said Glenda. "What a nice man, did you like him?"

"I did, he spoke a bit funny though, a bit slow, like Roy Rogers."

"They're both from America, that's the way they talk

over there."

"Can I go back to the golf tomorrow? It was great today, especially at the dunes."

"I'll speak to your Uncle George, I think he's going on Saturday, there's no fish selling in Dundee 'till Monday."

"We can get on the train ourselves Mum. Alec and Ian are going tomorrow."

"They've been saving their pocket money and helping out at the harbour while you've been playing football."

"I've been saving my pocket money."

"What pocket money?"

"I got it from Auntie Jean for getting extra beef from the butchers."

"How did you get extra beef?"

"I gave him a couple of cod I caught off the Harbour Wall."

Glenda laughed. "Ok Gary you win, remember though back here by 5.30, you've got the sea cadets at 7.00."

Next day, the three amigos arrived at Carnoustie to a totally different scene from the previous day. Grey sky, a sombre serious mood around the place.

The competition was started, and they instinctively knew they weren't going to meet Ben Hogan today. They weren't to know that they were destined never to meet him in person again.

Hogan went on to win at Carnoustie, becoming the only player to win the Masters, U.S. Open and Open Championship in the same year.

Back in Arbroath, the Three Amigos spent the rest of their summer holidays out at the local golf course at Elliot. Their love affair with the royal and ancient game had begun.

4

FORT WORTH TEXAS NOVEMBER 1953

Ben Hogan and his great friend Byron Nelson got together just after thanksgiving, to chat about golf and life.

"So Ben are you gonna retire now?"

Ben fixed Byron with one of his stares, cracked a smile and said, "Byron, you should know me by now, I'll never retire."

"Bob Jones retired after his greatest year. People are comparing your achievements to his."

"Retirement ain't in my nature, I'm a Texas man."

"So am I, and I retired 7 years ago."

Hogan laughed, "Yeah you were washed up anyway, you'd no choice!"

"Washed up! I'd just won 18 tournaments in '45."

"Exactly! You were all burned out, toast, fried, outta gas!"

Byron laughed, "yeah you're right, besides I'd always wanted to be a rancher."

"You got a pretty nice spread here."

"You know Ben, I've almost forgotten what my golfing life was like. Since I came out here, I've been totally immersed in this life."

"That's the Texan in you."

Byron laughed, "I guess you're right, you can take the man outa Texas, but you can't take Texas outa the man."

"Why that sounds almost poetic," laughed Ben.

The two men went outside for some air and a stroll, the early evening sun was still warm and the land hadn't yet succumbed to the chill of the north.

"You know Byron, ever since I got back from Carnoustie I've thinkin' about makin' a change, not that I want to become a rancher you understand, not unless you can train these longhorns to pick up the hundreds of balls I'm in the habit of hitting every day."

"No, I don't think they'd make very good caddies, they,"mooan" too much ha ha."

"Seriously though, my body's still suffering since the accident, I only managed 6 tournaments this year."

He bent to tie his shoe lace and stood again, straining a little as he straightened. "I do a bit of coachin', I get asked all the time to pass on what I've learned. I've always made notes when I've been praticin', so maybe I should write a book so that everyone can use my knowledge."

"Sounds like a great idea" said Byron, "maybe I'll do the same, pitch our two theories against each other."

"Great idea" said Ben, "means we can continue competing against each other."

THE FUNDAMENTAL TRUTH

"How will we know who wins?"

"We'll figure something out, we always do."

The pair of them laughed as they headed off into the sunset, they would talk till late, about their success, and how they'd achieved it.

The rivalry would endure.

5

ARBROATH JULY 1968

The three amigos were now 25 and their lives thus far had followed remarkably similar paths.

School had ended for them in 1959 and in those days academic excellence was merely a precursor to a life at sea. It was expected that young men from fishing backgrounds continued the tradition of following in their fathers' footsteps.

For these three friends that meant starting in one of their uncle's boats. In the early '60's most of the fishing boats in Arbroath were seine net vessels, pursuing the haddock.

This tasty North Sea inhabitant was the staple diet of the locals and of course, the foundation upon which the Arbroath Smokie export industry was built.

Gary and Alec learned their craft on such vessels, mostly out around the Bell Rock Lighthouse, where the haddock were to be found in abundance.

Ian, on the other hand worked on a small inshore boat called the Amber Queen owned by his uncle. Small line fishing was the main activity, where each of the crew would bring a baited line aboard.

The line had hundreds of hooks each with a mussel attached, line caught haddock always fetched top price at market.

THE FUNDAMENTAL TRUTH

By 1964 the men were well experienced and eager to try their own hand at running a vessel. An opportunity arose when Ian's Uncle Peter had to retire due to contracting Parkinson's disease.

The Amber Queen passed to Ian who had no hesitation in trying to persuade Gary and Alec to join him. Alec was keen as he'd been studying the fishing news and was keeping informed on a new market opening up with the demand for prawns.

The Amber Queen was converted to trawler and the three amigos commenced their pursuit of the scampi market in late 1964.

When the annual holidays came around in July '68 the three met for a game of golf at Elliot.

"Are we going up to Carnoustie next week to watch the Open?" asked Gary.

"I fancy going up for a practice day," said Ian.

"Me too," said Alec, "the crowds will be smaller and you'll see more shots."

"Ok," said Gary, "I'll take you up in my new beamer."

"Aye," laughed Ian, "easy to see the fishing's been going well."

"You earn it you spend it," said Gary.

"You just want to impress the girls," said Alec.

"That's true," said Gary, "and there'll be plenty to impress up at the Open. Anyway, you're one to talk; I hear you're moving up to the west end, bought one of those sandstone villas."

"True," said Ian, "I've always wanted a house with a garden that isn't made of concrete."

"What are you spending your money on Alec?" asked Gary.

"Need to know basis." said Alec tapping his nose.

"Wooo.. mysterious. What do you think Ian, is he saving for a new typewriter?"

"Probably saving to buy the Arbroath Herald. That's the company, not this week's edition. I think Alec fancies himself as Arbroath's version of Citizen Kane."

Alec smiled, "Ok you two, what's the stakes today?" He asked trying to change the subject.

All three were scratch golfers and had represented their area in inter district matches. Their work commitments however, prevented them from playing in national championships, which if they had, would probably have led to international recognition, such was the level of their skill.

"The usual," said Gary, "He who dares wins, and the winner gets to keep the claret jug for a week, suitably filled of course by the other two on a Saturday night."

"Are you two not getting fed up filling the jug with The Balvenie? By my count that's three weeks in a row. Does that not mean I get to keep it?" laughed Alec.

"You're due for a change of luck," said Ian, "the golf

THE FUNDAMENTAL TRUTH

course chooses its champion."

That was the key phrase. The battle then commenced.

It was a murky day when they set off for Carnoustie at 8.00 a.m. the following morning.

Typical of a day when the wind was off the sea, it was hard to tell, when looking at the horizon, where the sea ended and the sky started.

"We'll no see many high flying shots today," said Gary, "anything above 70ft will disappear into the clouds."

"The forecast says it'll brighten up later," said Ian. "I was hoping to get a look at Jack Nicklaus. They say he hits the ball so high it nearly goes into orbit."

"I read that," said Alec. "It said he hits a 1-iron higher than the other pros hit a 5-iron."

"Remember when we were here in '53," said Gary, "and we followed Ben Hogan round."

"How could we forget," said Alec, "he inspired us, follow your dreams and work hard he said and you can achieve anything."

"We've done not too bad so far," said Gary, "as he revved the engine of his new BMW Coupe.

"True," they agreed, "but this is only the start," said Ian.

"Anyway," said Gary, "we're on holiday and we don't want to talk about work."

"What does Ben Hogan do now?" asked Ian knowing that Alec would have the answer.

"As I've told the pair of you on many occasions," said Alec, "He rarely plays golf now, due to the injuries he received in the crash. He's heavily involved in his equipment business, making sure his club designs meet his exacting standards.

Then, of course, he is still in great demand doing demonstrations of the techniques illustrated in, 'The Book'."

"The Book" was none other than Hogan's book on the, "five lessons" When it was first published in 1957 it caused a sensation.

Beautifully illustrated and worded, anyone reading it for the first time, couldn't help but feel that Hogan was talking to them personally, walking with them step by step, to the promised land of a correct, powerful golf swing, that would repeat time after time.

Alec first discovered the book in the summer of '59 at the library in Arbroath, just after he'd left school for the last time. The three amigos had taken up golf in '54. Jack Stewart, the professional at Arbroath, was a great admirer of Hogan and had followed his career religiously.

Jack encouraged youngsters to take up the game, cutting down clubs and altering lies to suit the physique and age of the children.

In the spring of '54, during the school holidays, Gary's Uncle George had taken the three boys out to see Jack for their first lesson. When Alec told Jack about their encounter with Hogan at Carnoustie, the boys became his

THE FUNDAMENTAL TRUTH

special project.

Although Hogan hadn't written, "The Book" at that time Jack knew enough about the Hogan method to help his pupils on their journey. The three 11 year olds got started on the right lines and with Jack's help, would strengthen their
"fundamentals", year after year.

When Alec began to read, "The Book" he literally could not put it down. When he finished, he couldn't wait to tell the others, and when they couldn't put it down either, a meeting was called to discuss.

The 3 amigos were bonded even closer from that day, Hogan's fundamentals would guide them, for the rest of their lives.

The three amigos arrived at the car park at 8.15am and decided that they should get some breakfast before heading to the practice range.

The Caledonian Golf Club was open to non-members all year, the golfer's grill, which was a full Scottish breakfast, would certainly fit the bill.

"You need to get some lessons," said Alec as he surveyed the feast before him.

"I've read the book," said Gary.

"I mean cooking lessons," laughed Alec, "this is how the Amber Queen breakfast should look."

"You try frying an egg on a roller coaster," said Gary indignantly.

"All right children, let's eat," said Ian, and they did.

When the plates were cleaned and the tea was supped, the discussion moved on to the day's events.

"Do we know when he's going out on his practice round?" asked Gary.

"No but if we head across to the range all the players there will probably be going out within the hour, if he's there, we'll be able to go round with him and be back here in time for lunch," said Alec.

"Sounds like a plan," said Ian, so they went.

Gary Player was, as expected, hitting balls on the range. He was the golfer, identified by the friends as following the book's message the closest.

To GP (as he will henceforth be known due to the possible confusion, typically, 'Gary said to Gary' type of thing) Hogan was the Guru, the Chief, the Master of all things of a golfing nature and many other things besides.

The three amigos stood behind GP so they could study his move. There were barely half a dozen spectators watching the dozen or so players warming up.

He went through an array of shots, working through the bag, Alec was making notes. GP became aware of the three studying him. He finished his routine with a series of low flying pitches. Walking over smiling, GP introduced himself.

"Hello gentlemen, I've been expecting you."

Silence.

THE FUNDAMENTAL TRUTH

GP laughed, "Don't worry fellas I'm not the taxman."

GP explained how he and Hogan met frequently to discuss the evolution of the game of golf, and that the three amigos had many times, been a topic worthy of discussion. After many hand-shakes and back slapping the four headed to the first tee.

"Hogan told me to look out for you," said GP, "said you'd be of help to me as I prepared for this Championship."

"We'll do what we can," said Alec, "but you don't look like you need much help."

GP Laughed, "Don't you believe it Alec, we professional golfers are a superstitious breed. Every small detail can be the difference between success and failure."

GP, as was his nature had plenty to say to the three friends as they strode the fairways together. He enthused about aspects of Hogan's book and how he'd adapted the fundamentals to suit his own particular physique and unique mental approach.

The three marvelled at GP's dedication and determination to keep searching for improvement. They debated fleetingly whether they should abandon their fishing careers and immediately turn professional.

They laughed at the prospect. Although technically gifted and well qualified to attempt the life, GP's description of life on the road and in the air, of months away from home, sent collective shivers down their spines.

GP demonstrated all the skills on the golf course that

were required to navigate successfully around Carnoustie.

"Well gentlemen, what do you think?" asked GP as they walked off the 18th green.

"You'll need to guard against that tendency to hook," said Ian
"I know," said GP, "I've a tendency to hang back on my right side to counter my enthusiasm to use my fitness to the full."

"Legs and hips," said Alec.

"I know," laughed GP, "I'm like a coiled spring waiting to explode from the top, I'll need to cut back on the fingertip press-ups."

They parted then with words of hope and good luck.
"Time for lunch?" asked Alec.

"Caley Club?" asked Gary.

"Of course," said Ian.

After obtaining three pints of beer the three sat down to discuss the morning's events.

"Gary Player is certainly the heir apparent to Hogan at Carnoustie," said Gary.

"His course management is very similar," said Ian.

"He has the glint in his eye," said Alec.

"How did he know us?" asked Ian, "I mean, we only met Hogan the once, back in '53."

THE FUNDAMENTAL TRUTH

"Hogan's been taking an interest in our lives since I wrote to him in '62," said Alec.

The other two nodded, knowing that letters had been crossing the Atlantic from time to time.

"Now that our golf games have reached professional standard," said Alec, "Ben felt our experience of the Championship course, in all her moods, would help Gary in his quest to succeed him as a Carnoustie Open Champion."

Discussions continued over lunch, home-made steak pie, a nice change from the haddock staple, with cheese and oatcakes to finish.

"So what's on this afternoon?" asked Gary.

"Let's go and watch some of GP's rivals at the range, then if we like anyone we see, we'll head out with them on the course," said Alec.

When they got to the range, there were a few players doing their warm ups in preparation for a mid-afternoon start time. After a while they stepped away.

"Nearly all of these pros prefer to draw the ball," said Gary.

"They're very hands dominant," said Ian.

"Not so much the Americans" said Alec, "look at that man over there, see how he uses his legs and hips."

They went over for a closer look.

"That's Lee Trevino," said Alec, "he's just won the U.S. Open."

"Look where his feet are pointing," said Ian, "he fades everything."

"That's the best fade I've seen since Hogan," said Gary, "let's go follow him round." And they did.

By the 9th tee, the Three Amigos were the only people watching Trevino.

"That's the most beautiful adaptation of the book I've ever seen," said Alec. "Look at how he moves into the shot, he's like a cat stalking his prey, his feet are dancing even as he starts his backswing."

"That," said Ian, "is pure instinctive golf, half-way down he probably has 5 different shot options he could choose."

"One for each of the fundamentals," laughed Gary.

Trevino turned to them and smiled. "As a matter of fact, I probably have 20 options, problem is I normally pick the wrong one."

"Not on the evidence we've seen," said Gary.

"Why thank you sir, you're very kind," said Trevino.

The three amigos accompanied their new amigo the rest of the way round. They were treated to a wonderful display of shot-making.

Lee kept them entertained with constant dialogue

THE FUNDAMENTAL TRUTH

which covered his life story so far, laced with humour; he had opinions on everything, Mexicans, Americans, comedians, cars, women, tacos, golfers, even Hogan.

When they came off the course, they laughed their way back to the clubhouse. They needed a pint. They agreed, however, that despite all the hilarity, GP had a serious rival for the Open, if Trevino could choose the right shot at the right time, from his extensive library.

About 7pm they decided it was time to head home. The beamer was parked beyond the range. There was one player still on the range.

It was Jack Nicklaus. He was hitting a 3-wood into the westerly breeze. The sun was still quite high as it headed west. The first shot they heard, but couldn't follow.

"Shade your eyes and stand directly behind him," said Alec, there was no one else around. Having watched GP and Lee earlier on, they had a height in mind as they tried to pick up the flight of the ball.

"You need to look a lot higher," smiled Alec as he picked up the flight for the first time.

They watched in awe as each shot was dispatched into the stratosphere. Jack continued to hit each shot with meticulous preparation, as if the Open itself was on the line.

After half an hour Jack was finished and he turned to speak to the three, who had remained silent throughout.

"Hi fellas, appreciate your quiet and concentration, I hope I didn't bore you with all those fades I've been hitting."

"Those were fades?" asked Gary. "They flew so far and high I couldn't tell."

"I couldn't either," laughed Jack, "I'm just out here working on my stock fade. I'm pretty sure I had it though, from the feel on the face."

"I saw a fade," laughed Alec. "It went so far it faded out of sight."

"I guess." laughed Jack. "It's a small ball after all."

"Is the fade going to be your preferred shape this week?" asked Ian.

"It nearly always is. Depends on the wind - I may have to hit it a little lower."

"What do you think of Carnoustie?" asked Alec.

Jack fixed his sharp blue eyes on Alec for a moment that was a little stretched, before answering.

"The golf course is very fair, a little flatter than I normally prefer, but the hazards are all out in the open, so the strategy is dictated by the strength and direction of the wind."

"That's exactly what Ben Hogan told us in 1953," said Alec.

"You spoke to Hogan in '53?" asked Jack incredulously, knowing that these three young men would be but kids back then.

"Certainly did," said Gary, "he gave us some great advice."

"I'd like to hear some of that advice," said Jack, "would you fellas care to join me for a beer?"

"Of course," said Gary, "the Caley has a lovely selection of ales."

And so they went.

Four days later...

14th Hole.

"Hogan never offered me that kind of advice," said GP.

"Maybe he felt you didn't need it, you were a lot older than these kids when you first met Hogan," said Jack.

The pair of them were walking down the fairway, chatting as the good friends they were. Although one of them was destined to be Open Champion that day. It was a normal day at the office for these great professionals.

"Maybe Jack's right," thought GP as the ball left the face of his 4-wood.

The three amigos were standing to the left of the green as GP's ball landed just short of the green and made its way to within 4ft of the pin.

"That shot probably won Gary his second Open," said Alec.

"I agree," said Ian, "the golf course seems to be favouring Gary, see how the first bounce was quite high, as if the course was inviting the ball to look for the best route to the hole.

The second bounce gave it real purpose as it eased left and accelerated slightly on its new path."

When GP climbed past the spectacles and could see where his ball had finished, he had a surge of adrenalin. As fit as he was, he knew he'd have to manage that if he was to sink the putt.

A smattering of applause greeted him onto the green. He noticed the Three Amigos over to the left, smiling and applauding.

He touched the rim of his hat in acknowledgement. This small gesture allowed him to re-focus and hole the putt for an eagle 3.

The lead was his; he would not lose it…

After the presentation and press questions, GP caught up with the three amigos and thanked them for their support.

Alec spoke for the three of them when he said, "What a terrific display of shot selection and execution, that was tough conditions, added to by a certain Mr. Nicklaus breathing down your neck."

"You know fellas," said GP, "The people you play with can either inspire you or diminish you, playing with my good friend Jack brought out the very best in me. I consider this victory as my greatest in golf."

No one was arguing.

6

AUGUSTA GEORGIA NOVEMBER 1968

"Tell me about your strategy Gary," asked Ben.

"It was pretty cold Ben," said Gary, "so the ball wasn't carrying far, but there was plenty of run."

"Reminds me of '53," laughed Ben, "do they never have summer in Scotland?"

"They do have long days," said Dwight. "I remember the summer of '44, June 6th was a very long day."

The others stared at Dwight for a moment, he was deep in thought.

Ben, Byron, Gary and Dwight had a good going fourball underway as they approached Amen Corner.

"I played practice rounds in the company of our mutual friends." said GP. "Their knowledge of Carnoustie is second to none. They seem to know every landing spot for every wind direction and shot shape."

Ben Laughed, "Wow that's impressive memory, given they were only 10 at the time."

"I think they've learned a few of their own Ben," laughed GP, "They do play the course every week, rain or shine, summer and winter. The temperature on the coast can be just 2 or 3 degrees colder in December than June, if the wind is from the south west.

The advice they gave me was invaluable, Jack had similar knowledge having bought the amigos a few beers in the Caley Club on the Sunday night.

They'd let it slip out that they'd spoken to you in '53 and you know Jack, meticulously prepared, especially for the Majors. I had my work cut out that day for sure."

Augusta's greens were still pretty slick so the pins were located generously. Dwight had his usual stroke per hole, plus 9 extra for the additional putts.

Today he was paired with Byron and the duo were dovetailing well to be 2 up at the turn.

Gary and Ben turned to look at Dwight who said, "today may be even longer if I continue to play this well, I may stay out here all night."

"You're gonna have to if you think two up at the turn is gonna end up in a victory" laughed Ben.

"I've got a plane to catch," said Gary.

"Don't worry Gary we'll have this match wrapped up by 15," said Byron.
No more on '68 strategy was said as the 4 got on with the serious business at hand. 11th fairway, all four players had hit good drives. Dwight was away at 200 yards from the green.

"I think I'll lay-up in my usual spot," he said.

"Smart move," said Gary, "you've got 2 shots on this hole. It'd be a shame if you went for it and dumped it in the water."

THE FUNDAMENTAL TRUTH

"I don't think you laid up on June 6th," said Ben.

"That was my job," protested Dwight.

"This is your job now," said Ben.

"I thought this was just a game," said Dwight.

"The game of life," said Ben.

Dwight knew the game so he laid up in his usual spot.

The three pros continued to trade blows all the way up to 15 where Bob Jones came out to meet them. He was not well enough to walk any more, but was able to buzz around Augusta in his buggy.

"How's it going fellas," he said, "looks like you're having a good match."

"We're all playing second fiddle to Dwight here," said Byron, "I've never seen him play this well. We're 2 up, Ben and Gary ain't too pleased."

Bob looked over to Ben who was deep in conversation with Gary.

"Break it up you two," laughed Bob, "Dwight's all ready to hit."

Sure enough, Dwight had already teed up and was sizing up his options as he gazed over the water to the 16th green.

There was no wind to speak of so the water was like a sheet of glass. When Ben and Gary arrived, Dwight was still staring, seemingly transfixed.

"What's up Dwight?" asked Byron, "It's a 7-iron for you, all day long."

Dwight seemed to wake up at the sound of his name.
"Sorry partner," he said, "I got a little distracted, yeah you're right, let's put these two bantam weights on the canvas."

Back in the club-house, the Glenlivet had been duly poured.

"Well played Dwight, cheers" said Ben.

"What about me?" beamed Byron.

"You did contribute on 17," agreed Gary.

"Dwight was having his usual tree trouble, so I figured a par would be good enough to take care of you guys."

Gary and Ben who had been doubled up with laughter, as Dwight wrestled with his tree, agreed. "We were in no fit state to argue," laughed Ben.

Dwight sat quietly sipping his Glenlivet, seemingly drifting in some far off place.

"That tree talks to me," he said in a matter of fact tone.

"I'm not surprised given the amount of advice that you offer it," said Ben.

"I guess I am a bit loud," said Dwight," I'm always apologising for shouting at that tree for hitting my ball. Anyway the tree talks to me long before I get to the 17th tee. It starts whispering as I leave the 15th green."

"That's probably why you usually mess up the 16th," said Gary.

"You're thinking too far ahead," said Byron.

"What were you thinking on the morning of June 6th?" asked Ben trying to change the subject.

"Pretty much what Bob Jones told me back in early '44. He described the tactics for poker and golf, and how they could be applied to the invasion of Normandy." He paused and then continued.

"You made your plans, worked on your strategy, practiced your moves, studied your opponents, set up your bluffs, chose your options and committed fully to the execution."

"Wow! Golf, poker and army manoeuvres. It's the same game," said Ben.

"Pretty much," said Dwight, "just on a different scale, with more players."

"People don't die playing golf and poker," said Gary.

"Not physically," smiled Byron," but we all die a little with every lip-out."

"Let's go see Bob" said Ben, "we need to discuss this further over lunch."

And they did.

7

AUGUSTA GEORGIA APRIL 1972

"Welcome Bob" said Dwight," I've been waiting for you since
I passed into 'this world'."

It was 3.00 am in the lounge of the Augusta National Golf Club. The date was 2nd April 1972.

"Hello Dwight my friend," said Bob "how long have you been waiting?"

"Only three years," laughed Dwight, "time don't matter where we are now."

"I'm sure glad you're here to welcome me," said Bob, "I wasn't sure what to expect when I walked through these doors like this for the first time."

"It's an amazing feeling isn't it? I've been walking the golf course every day since my first masters back in '69." His eyes were wide with excitement.

"I've been busy ever since discovering how we can interact with the real world," said Dwight.

"Do tell," laughed Bob.

So he did.

"I think we can have a lot of fun making mischief here at the Masters," said Dwight.

THE FUNDAMENTAL TRUTH

"Why don't we set up a committee?" said Bob, "kind of like a club within a club, so to speak, membership by invitation only of course." They both laughed.

"I was over at St. Andrews last month and I bumped into Old Tom Morris. He told me they've been running such a committee at the Open since 1921."

"They started with a committee of 5, Old Tom, Young Tom, Willie Park, Jamie Anderson and Bob Ferguson. All of them had won the Open at least three times and that was the criteria by which eligibility for membership could be achieved."

"I think I was the first real victim of their mischief making when I took three shots in a bunker and promptly walked off the course," laughed Bob. "Old Tom told me it was Willie Park's mischief when each time my ball hit the face of the bunker and rebounded into my footprint."

He smiled: "Willie was old school. He felt at 19, I needed a lesson in humility, before I could fully appreciate the finer points of links golf. He was right."

And so it began at Augusta, the pair of them wandering the fairways making mischief wherever and whenever they saw fit.

Mischief making at Augusta that year was easy as the greens were infested with Poa Annua; a terrible weed which plagued Augusta's surfaces from time to time.

Players were three putting everywhere, but the pair of them felt sorry for the players who were frustrated and blamed the course condition.

Bob and Dwight felt that this wasn't mischief in the

spirit of the game as it removed the best putters' skills from their list of weapons.

Jack Nicklaus managed himself best that week and gained his 4th Green Jacket.

The committee did make their mark, however, on day two of the tournament. The victim was none other than 4 time winner, Arnold Palmer.

It was on the 9th hole.

"What do you think Bob?" asked Dwight.

"Well Dwight," said Bob, "Arnie's Army, as normal, is huge and is seen by everyone as being an advantage against the rest of the field. Whether it be a huge roar when he holes a putt, or an errant shot bouncing off the masses into a more favourable position than the shot deserved. Let's see how he copes with a negative effect of his Army."

Arnold had missed the green to the right and his ball had come to rest in a depression made by a folding chair.

"Surely I get relief from that?" asked Arnold. "I believe the chair was used by an official and is therefore a movable obstruction."

The question was put to the rules committee. In the meantime Arnold completed the 9th hole with both the original ball and a provisional ball, pending the ruling.

When the decision was reached and Arnold informed, he was standing on the 12th tee.

The ruling from the committee confirmed that there

would be no relief.

"I don't agree," said Arnold, "but I have to accept the ruling."

Bob smiled at Dwight. "Looks like his balance is a little on tilt," said Bob knowing that Dwight would appreciate the poker reference.

"I agree," said Dwight. "The swing hath no fury like a Palmer scorned."

Palmer selected an 8-iron, the swing was a blur, the ball settled in the front bunker.

Another slash, the ball sailed over the green, marching quickly with the same club, he repeated the swing, ball back in bunker, another slash, a missed 3ft putt and a 6 was entered on the card.

"Now that's what I call mischief," laughed Dwight. "The golf course chooses her champion, she and no-one's army."

8

ARBROATH   JULY   1975

"I think I'm going to leave the boat and go to work on the Riggs," said Gary.

North Sea oil had just stated to flow into the UK and there were many new opportunities for people to work in what was rumoured to be a very exciting and rewarding industry.

The UK had entered the common market in 1970. The ensuing 5 years had proved progressively more difficult for fishermen in Arbroath, due in the main to the removal of national fishing boundaries.

This allowed all Common Market countries unfettered access to the Scottish fishing grounds.

Fish stock preservation was becoming a major political issue. Quotas on certain species were starting to appear. Fishermen were starting to dump perfectly marketable fish back in the sea just so they wouldn't exceed "the quota".

This was anathema to communities up and down the nation.

Fishermen daily put their lives at risk to bring this valuable food source to the Nation. Many hard working people became "criminals" as they landed perfectly good fish on the black market.

Although the Amber Queen had thrived during this period given that they had diversified, the crew were well aware of the threat to their future livelihood.

Ian had been particularly aggrieved when Brussels passed a law which stated that all fishing boats over the length of 40ft required railings to be fitted in order to prevent fishermen falling overboard.

"Obviously," Ian said at the time, "Brussels thinks it's ok to fall overboard from a 39ft. boat".

The cost at the time of the work to fit the railings to the beautiful 45ft. long Amber Queen and all the other health and safety requirements was prohibitive.

Pro-active as ever, Ian chopped 5ft. 4in off her bough for a fraction of the cost.

"Fishing in the North Sea is a dangerous business" he said after the work was completed. "The people who choose to go there, accept the risks. The Amber Queen at mid-ship, lies only 4ft above the water line. To add another 2 tons to the super-structure would make her less stable in adverse weather. We've cut the bow for all our safety."

"I'm thinking of becoming a journalist" said Alec. "I love writing and all this interference from Brussels has got my dander up."

Ian sat quietly for a moment looking at the pair of them.
"The fishing's been good to us all" he said finally we've made a lot of money and we've had a lot of laughs."

Nods of agreement.

"We've come through a few scrapes together, in many ways, were lucky to still be here. The rigs won't be any picnic either Gary, there will be other dangers lurking out there."

"I know," said Gary, "but the riches on offer, make the risks worthwhile and of course I'd be working 2 weeks offshore, leaving me 2 weeks free for other activities, hee-hee."

They all laughed.

"We're all 32 now and none of us are married" said Gary, "or have any kids. I know we've had a few close calls but the sea makes it hard these days to get into relationships. This is the seventies remember and the number of ladies out there aspiring to be wives of fishermen is diminishing faster than the cod stocks."

They sat for a moment.

"Let's go to Carnoustie" said Ian, "the Open's back in town"
And so they went.

****

The usual suspects were back at Carnoustie looking to add to their hall of major championships. Gary Player was defending the title he won at Lytham last year.

Jack Nicklaus was the undisputed no.1 player in the world and was this year's Masters Champion.

Lee Trevino was the reigning P.G.A. champion and all three had arrived early to prepare. It was early on Sunday, when they teed off together for a practice round.

"Do you remember the last time we played here?" asked Gary.

"Vaguely," said Jack. "It didn't turn out too well for me."

"Sorry to remind you my friend," said Gary, "being here again reminds me of the feelings I was experiencing that Sunday afternoon."

"Do tell," said Lee "I love a sentimental journey."

"I think we all agree that Carnoustie offers the toughest but fairest test of your abilities of all the Open venues."

Jack and Lee both nodded.

"The fairways are generous and accept a drive without shooting it forward, sideways, or even backwards as we've all experienced elsewhere."

Again, nods all round.

"The bunkering is superb and the approaches to the greens generally allows you the option of feeding the ball into them if the wind conditions favour that type of shot, the exceptions being 3 and 18."

The nods continued.

"When Hogan won here in '53 he told me he felt the golf course wanted him to win."

Jack looked at Lee who smiled but uniquely for him, didn't say a word.

"What you're saying Gary, is that Hogan believed the golf course helped him to win."

"That's correct Jack, Hogan observed how the ball reacted each time it hit the ground and it matched his expectations almost every time, given the knowledge of the type of shot he had just hit."

"We all hope for a good first bounce, but we accept that bad bounces do occur, that's just golf," said Jack.

"Me, I just hope for any kind of bounce, means I haven't flown into a bush or a bunker," laughed Lee.

"What helped me in '68 was that I truly believed the golf course wanted me to win," said Gary. "I mean you were charging Jack as only you can, but I was able to stay calm, fully expecting things to go my way."

"Why do you think the golf course chose you as opposed to me or anyone else for that matter?" asked Jack.

"The golf course certainly chose me back in '72" said Lee, "remember Muirfield and what happened to Tony (Jacklin)."

"How could we forget," Gary and Jack said in unison.

"I'd hacked my way through the back of 17 in 4 said to Tony it's all yours as I walked by him just short in 2.

He pitched on to about 15ft and I said to Willie, 'Gimme a club.' I took no time in hitting my 5th which, as you know, went in."

"Maybe it was because you had let go that the golf course helped you," said Gary.

"There's a lot in what you say, Gary," said Jack, "my strategy always revolves around giving up control to gain control. I always played my best golf when my mind was free and I was acting on instinct."

"Let's chat further after the game" said Lee. "I want to know how the golf course will choose me more often, I got bills to pay."

"Let's go to the Caley club for lunch, I've got a feeling we may bump into some old friends," said Gary.

The three amigos were having a beer when the golfers walked into the lounge. After greetings were exchanged, they all sat down to lunch. The discussion as always, eventually gravitated to their favourite topic.

"Hogan's here," said GP matter-of-factly.

They all looked at him, it was well known that Hogan, who was now in his 60's rarely left Texas never mind cross the Atlantic.

"So is Byron." Stunned looks all around.

"What are you saying Gary that they're here in spirit, kind of like whispering in the wind," said Alec.

"No," laughed GP, "they're here in Scotland, although not in Carnoustie, at the moment. They went up north for a few days with a young American pro, Tom Watson."

He ignored the looks on the surrounding faces. "Byron is coaching him and Ben is helping on strategy. I believe they are playing links courses and drinking malt whisky."

"Sounds like fun," said Lee, "do you know when they're coming down?"

"I think he said Tuesday at the latest. Depends on how much they're enjoying themselves. Tom Watson must be highly rated if Byron and Ben felt it important enough to leave their beloved Texas."

"He is," said Jack, "he's got the perfect game for links golf, he moves it both ways with ease and he's got a terrific short game."

Meanwhile up north, Byron and Ben were following Tom around the Royal Dornoch Links. They had acquired a buggy for the task to help preserve the joints for warmer climes.

"This is the first time I've been back since '53," said Ben. "I've never been this far north."

"Me neither," said Byron, "this is golf in its rawest form. The elements, the topography, shot making examination of the highest order."

"Tom looks to be coping well with the conditions," said Ben.

"So my more upright swing plane philosophy meets with your approval" laughed Byron.

"It certainly suits Tom's physical attributes," said Ben. "My fundamentals can be applied to all physiques," he laughed, "even yours. A body swing is a body swing."

The following Monday Tom Watson was lifting the Claret Jug after an 18 hole playoff with Australian Jack Newton.

THE FUNDAMENTAL TRUTH

Watching the ceremony on the BBC in the comfort of their rented farmhouse, Ben cracked open the Glenmorangie.

"Have a sniff" he said, "certainly different from Speyside."

Clinking crystal, the toast was: "Tom Watson, champion golfer of the year, first of many I think," said Byron.

"Tom learned a lot about himself this week," said Ben, "acceptance is the greatest skill a golfer can possess."

9

AUGUSTA   GEORGIA   APRIL 1986

"How about Jack?" enthused Byron.

"The golf course chooses its champion," echoed Ben, "Seve listened to the whispering wind on 15 - told him it was Jack's time."

"Agreed," said Byron, "there's something about this place, it's almost cathedral like, especially back nine on Sunday."

The roar that greeted Jack's eagle on 15 shook the trees to their very roots, the rest of the field were adversely affected by it.

Jack, on the other hand, the 46 year old Jack, got such a boost of adrenalin he must have felt 20 years younger.

"The patrons become part of the fabric of the place, when they hold their breath, the players feel the tension, when they roar, the players jump, then let their breath go."

"Bob must be smiling today" said Ben.

Somewhere near the 15th green, he was.

10

ARBROATH   JULY   1999

Gary said to his 17 year old son, also Gary: "Who do you think will the Open next week?"

(There's a danger we're going to have too many Garys in this story, so to help keep confusion to a minimum, from now on Gary's son will be known as Young Gary Shepherd or YGS. Gary's Dad will be known as Auld Gary Shepherd or AGS. Gary Player will still be known as Gary Player or GP).

"Tiger," YGS said without hesitation.

AGS was home from the North Sea where he worked 2 weeks on, 2 weeks off. He liked to golf when he was off and as his son was finished school they'd be playing together regularly over the summer. The sun was warm on their backs this particular evening, the sky a vibrant array of purple hues and warm sandstone shades.

"I know Tiger's the favourite but he's yet to show form on links land. With the wet summer the rough is penal, some people are calling it 'Carnasty.'"

"He's the best Dad."

"He's the number 1, of that there is no doubt, and Augusta definitely chose him in '97."

"How do you mean, 'chose him'?"

"A wise man once told me that the golf course chooses

its champion. Let me explain." AGS took the opportunity to wipe down his golf balls with the damp cloth hanging from his gold bag. "You've been playing golf now for 9 years Gary and you managed to win a trophy or two along the way. Have you ever noticed on these days that things happened slightly differently on the course?"

"Yes Dad, I holed a lot of putts!"

"Were these putts of a length you expected to hole?"

"Well, anything under 20ft," YGS smiled.

His Dad laughed. "The joys of being young. So you expected to hole these and accepted the result whether they went in or not?"

"Obviously."

"That's what I mean. In essence, the golf course chooses which putts go in, which bunkers you bounce over etc. etc."

"Dad, I know all this, I've been playing golf for 9 years, I know all about accepting bad breaks and good breaks with impunity, you taught me."

"So, knowing what you know, why do you think Tiger will win this week?"

"Why do you think he won't?"

"The weather forecast is for cold and wet conditions, Carnoustie will demand a cultured approach - she won't be overpowered."

"Who do you think will win?"

THE FUNDAMENTAL TRUTH

"The last three Carnoustie champions were Watson, Player and Hogan, all three were terrific wind players. Watson still is but his putting isn't what it was. It really is an open championship this year."

"Ok Dad, when are we going up to watch?"

"I've arranged to go with Alec and Ian on Sunday, there's lots of former champions there to entertain us."

"Cool."

****

Alec Cargill had come a long way since his deckhand days on the Amber Queen. Staying true to his dream, he became a journalist, moving up to Aberdeen where there was a lot going on with the Oil and Fishing industries.

Alec had always been interested in Politics and found plenty to fill the column inches. He had a reputation for straight talking, searching for the truth, which those in power feared, but respected.

After 24 years however, and at the age of 56 he needed a change. He was inspired (some say conspired) to run, and was duly elected as an independent member of the new Scottish Parliament. Unmarried and with no children, it was easy for him to sell up and move near his constituents in Arbroath.

Ian Beattie had never left Arbroath although he had moved his family to the west end of town. His wife Elaine who was a history teacher and their 3 daughters, Karen, Christine and Louise enjoyed life in the large rooms and gardens of the 19th century sandstone villa.

I. A. SHEPHERD

He was still fishing the Amber Queen, but knew that when his current crew left, (normally for the oil rigs and the black gold) he would probably retire to the golf course.

Being members of Carnoustie links, Alec, Ian, Auld Gary and Young Gary had access to other local courses during the Open period.

A hastily convened match between the four was due to start over Elliot Links, at 12.00 on Saturday.

The Pro at Elliot was a Carnoustie native. Lindsay Ewart knew the four well, he kept them well supplied with the latest equipment.

Young Gary had been practising and was now chatting to Lindsay, awaiting the arrival of the other three.

"Have you seen the latest driver from Taylor Made" said Lindsay who was a stockist. "The ball looks like a pea in front of the face."

YGS studied the club. "I don't see much difference from mine," he said, "it was new only 6 months ago."

"The speed you generate Gary, you should give it a go," said Lindsay, "this is a demo, take it out today, you'll impress the old boys. You never know, if you knock it 20 yards past your Dad he may buy you one."

"More likely, he'll buy it for himself," laughed YGS, "he won't like it if I out-drive him."

Meanwhile, in the car park, two amigos crossed to meet one another.

THE FUNDAMENTAL TRUTH

"Good to see you Alec," said Ian as they shook hands, "big changes since May."

"You could say," laughed Alec, "who'd have thought a fisherman's son from Arbroath would end up an MSP."

"You're well thought of in the town Alec. The support you gave the fishermen in their fight against the quotas of Brussels has not been forgotten."

"Thanks Ian, I certainly wrote from experience, the injustices heaped on our fishing communities fired my interest in politics. The 1000's of perfectly good dead fish dumped back in the sea on a daily basis just made me angry. The fish market in Arbroath has been closed for years, the fleet is decimated, all as a result of the Common Fisheries Policy," said Ian.

"True," said Alec, "that's gone and won't be coming back. Nearly all the fish are landed at Peterhead now. The fishing capacity up there has to be seen to be believed, fewer in number but far more efficient in their catching capabilities."

"So my friend," said Ian, "what's going to be driving you forward on your political crusade?"

"The oil boom in Aberdeen was good to me and the country of course, providing a lot of former fishermen and communities with gainful employment."

The two waved politely at a foursome leaving the 18th and heading for the clubhouse.

"I learned a lot about the power of oil as a driving force in the economy and its huge impact on the environment. The planet's climate is being adversely affected and without doubt is the major issue facing us all, going forward. The big question for me is: what happens after the oil runs out?"

"I'll come and work for you," piped up AGS, "I'm getting too old for North Sea exposure"!

They headed for the tee.

"Are we gonna tee off sometime today?" asked YGS patiently waiting on the tee, "while we're still young, or should I say, while I'm still young ha-ha."

The match commenced. Despite YGS trying to focus on the game and get the others to follow suit, the three amigos continued to talk about politics and YGS could hear them, slowly but surely, develop a plan, a plan for the future, a plan that would shape not only their future, but the future of mankind.

The match ended. A low scoring affair with Young Gary holing his standard 20 footer for a birdie on 18 to secure victory.

"Nice driver son," said AGS, "and no, tell Lindsay I'm not tempted, a lot of money for a marginal gain."

"20 yards further isn't marginal" said YGS.

"You're getting older and stronger son, I'm getting older and weaker. It's not the equipment. Time waits for no man."

Back in the clubhouse the chat had moved on to the upcoming Open.

"So," asked YGS, "who's going to win?"

THE FUNDAMENTAL TRUTH

Ian replied first. "I like Justin Leonard - he won two years ago at Troon, he's a Hogan disciple and he's from Texas."

"Good call," said Alec, "he's got to be up there given the tightness of the course. All the great Europeans are getting a bit long in the tooth, Faldo was the last major winner and that was in '96. I think O'Meara could defend, what about you Gary and don't say the golf course will decide!"

"I agree. The old guard don't quite have what it takes if the wind blows. Ernie and Monty look good bets to me. Young Gary here can't see past Tiger, but I don't see it myself."

"I don't feel it will be an American this time, they've won the last four."

****

Much later that night in the Caley Club snooker room…

Chairman of the,"Open Championship Mischief Makers Committee", Old Tom Morris welcomed the members to the 128th Open. The committee comprised 13 members dating back to the first Open Champion in 1860, Willie Park Snr.

"Gentlemen," opened Old Tom. "It falls to me as your chairman, to open these proceedings in the time honoured fashion."

He leapt onto the snooker table with his trusty putter in hand and stroked three putts with the minimum of fuss into the top left hand pocket, each putt holed being greeted with roars and stamping of feet. The hands raised the single malt filled Quaich. The meeting was declared open.

"First order of business is to announce that we have a new member to welcome into our midst. This is indeed auspicious times for our committee as for the second year running we welcome a Grand Slam winner." Cheers and stamping of feet.

"Following Ben here back at Birkdale, it gives me great pleasure to welcome Gene, "The Squire" Sarazen. The door swung open and in walked Gene fully resplendent in New York Yankee pinstripe plus fours.

"I thought it was Babe Ruth," laughed Bobby Jones.

"I thought it was the chef bringing desert" laughed The Haig.

Uproar and mayhem.

"Order gentlemen," said Old Tom, "Gene, welcome to the Open Championship Mischief Makers Committee."

"As tradition dictates we now call on you to say a few words."

"Thank you Mr Chairman" said Gene, "what a fine body of men, or should that be a gathering of ghosts, or should that be a plethora of poltergeists, or should that be a summation of spirits, let's just say a melee of mischief makers."

THE FUNDAMENTAL TRUTH

Tapping of Quaich and stamping of feet.

"If I knew it was such a formal occasion I'd have dressed a little differently but as the only New Yorker here I thought I'd liven things up a bit if you'll excuse the pun." Chuckles.

"The Yankees are always up to mischief in the Bronx so I thought, as a rookie, the outfit would give me confidence to perform at my best."

"I'm not lookin' to hit a home run first time out, maybe a couple of bunts or a stolen base perhaps."

"This is golf, it's The Open, not The World Series," laughed The Haig.

"Really!" said The Squire, "Looks like an over grown pool table to me."

"It's a snooker table, and they don't bunt or steal bases on it either, they screw and stun."

Uproar.

"Gentlemen, gentlemen," said Old Tom, "If we can move on to the next order of business for today's proceedings: the allocation of holes."

"Tradition dictates that former winners at the year's venue have priority. Henry Cotton, as the 1937 winner here at Carnoustie, has the first choice."

"Thank you Mr. Chairman" said Henry, "I like 16 as I think it is the most demanding tee shot: a long iron downwind and a well hit driver when the wind is off the sea. The target is narrow and offers plenty of opportunity for mischief making."

"Thank you Henry," said old Tom. "Ben?"

"If I may Mr. Chairman" said Ben "I'd quite like to be at 18, it's where the pressure is the greatest with the Barry Burn winding around and out of bounds all down the left."

"Excellent Ben," said Old Tom, "remember though as a Grand Slam Champion you may choose two holes on which to make mischief."

"Very well" said Ben, "In that case I'll take 17 as well, I love water and as they are adjacent they're easy to cover. I do note, however, that my legs work a lot better now than they used to." Laughter

"Now that we have 3 Grand Slam winners on our committee, along with 11 other qualified members, I believe that leaves only 1 hole without a resident mischief maker.

Great news, especially on the final two days after the cut when the early hole residents can make for the beer tent after the leaders go past." Much tapping of quaichs and stamping of feet.

"Ok gentlemen, let the bidding commence." Uproar!

After half an hour the uproar was tailing off and apart from the odd skirmish between Bob Ferguson and Jamie Anderson, things were calming down.

They always fought over hole no.1 no matter where the Open was held. It was agreed by the committee that these

THE FUNDAMENTAL TRUTH

two alternate holes 1 and 2.

The Great Triumvirate always settled among themselves which of them took holes 3, 4 and 5.

No one argued with Willie Park who always confirmed, "I'll take no.6."

Old Tom and Young Tom agreed on 7 and 8. With all the winners before the Great War satisfied, the remaining 7 holes would be allocated between 4 players.

Bob and Gene as Grand Slam winners took 12, 13, 14 and 15 respectively, "The Haig" wanted 10 as it had its own beer tent, leaving, "Old Baggy Pants" Bobby Locke the choice of 9 or 11. He chose 11 leaving 9 as the floater.

"Ok gentlemen," said Tom, "thank you for that, "The Haig" as always is in charge of club house mischief, although on this occasion I believe he has 6 to choose from, and one of them is exclusively for ladies. Who knows what he'll get up to there. He may need volunteers to help." Uproar!

"Final piece of formal business gentlemen, the review of our qualification procedures. Currently we have two methods by which membership of this committee can be achieved.
These are :- 1) Winner of 3 Open Championships.
2) Winner of The Grand Slam.

With Gene's arrival our membership has swelled to 14 and at the present moment there are 7 others currently eligible to join us when their time comes. If we are all agreed to preserve the qualification rules as they are please show your approval in the usual manner. 'AYE' roared all present.

"Thank you gentlemen" said Tom, "that concludes the formalities.

Gene, if you don't mind, please select one of our excellent malts in order that we may commence the informalities."

"My pleasure," said Gene as he selected a 15 year old Glenlivet. The cheers resounded.

****

Sunday morning came and the three amigos and YGS headed off to Carnoustie by train, the ten minute journey without car parking problems was an easy decision and reminded them of the first time they went to the Open in '53.

"The trains were much different then," said Alec to YGS who was fascinated by the legend of Hogan. "We had individual compartments and were driven by a steam engine. We were quite near the front of the train and the noise as it was leaving the station was incredible.

I remember thinking as we left the platform that this was the most exciting thing we had ever done, the three of us off on a real adventure, the shuddering train felt so huge and powerful, we had no control over it.

When it deposited us at Carnoustie, we watched it leave with a tinge of sadness. That soon passed though when we realised we were on our own, that day, was the longest day of our lives, the day we met Ben Hogan."

"What was he like?" asked YGS.

THE FUNDAMENTAL TRUTH

"He was very wise" said Alec. "When he spoke to us we were silent, which for your Dad was a major achievement! We could have listened to him all day. He knew what it was like to grow up without a Dad. That day, that journey, had a huge influence on our lives and we're still reaping the benefits to this day." The other two nodded.

9.00 a.m. on Sunday, Carnoustie was eerily quiet and unlike in '53, the three amigos and YGS had arrived without a picnic.

The Caley Club, however, with its "Full Scottish" would satisfy their needs.

"Have you checked the draw for today's practice?" asked Alec.

"Yes" said Ian, "Tiger and O'Meara went out at 6.30, we should be able to pick them up around the 15th once we've had breakfast."

"Breakfast can wait," said YGS as he went out the door.

The three amigos laughed as the door closed behind him.

"He really is hooked on Tiger," said AGS.

"As is the entire golfing world," laughed Alec.

"He is a very gifted golfer," confirmed Ian," the game has moved on a long way since '75 , no more persimmon heads, the new golf balls are amazing, Tiger's swing speed is incredible, fitness is much more relevant now as it helps maximise the benefits of the new technology."

"There's a certain Mr Player who'd argue that fitness has always been relevant" laughed Alec.

"True," the others agreed.

"Do you think Hogan's fundamentals are no longer relevant?" asked Alec with a smile.

"No," laughed Ian, "humans still have arms, legs, hips and feet the last time I looked."

"Exactly." said Gary. "Hogan's fundamentals will always apply, especially the move" they all nodded in silence.

"I was sad to see the passing of Ben a couple of years back," said Ian, "I suppose he'll have taken up residence beside his bridge at Augusta."

"I don't know," said Gary, "it's pretty quiet down there, I think he could be here, there's more wind here, plenty of entertainment throughout the year with all the American and overseas visitors."

"You could be right" said Alec, "Augusta's a pretty quiet place outside of Masters week. He probably just goes back once a year to catch up with old friends.

Carnoustie's very rarely quiet, did you see where they put the plaque to commemorate Hogan's victory in '53.

"Yes," laughed Gary, "on the 6th tee right beside the army snipers' range."

"You know" said Alec, "I've watched these snipers from the Buddon course, lying down like a bunch of seals sunning themselves, casually picking off targets at 1000 yards, Hogan would be impressed"!

The breakfast was finished in silence.
"We should try and catch up with GP." said Gary, "When is he going out?"

"11.00am" said Ian, "he's going out with Ernie and Nicky Price."

"Ok let's go" said Alec, "I'll bet he's on the range."

As they left the clubhouse and walked past the 18th green they could see young Gary watching Tiger and O'Meara tee off on 17, they waved and got a thumbs up back.

As expected GP was on the range warming up.

"Still looking great isn't he?" said Ian as they approached the fence. GP was still swinging with great athletic ability at the age of 63, Ernie Els and Nick Price were either side of him and the contrast was something to behold.

Ernie, a large man, had a swing so tranquil, the illusion of speed was almost hypnotic. He caressed the ball 300 yards through the air. Nick, also a big man, had a very brisk action; you could almost imagine he could hit 2 shots in the time Ernie took to hit one.

"This is a good study for the purist," said Alec as they watched the display of shot-making par excellence. After 20 minutes they were finished, GP looked over and spotted the three amigos.

"Well hello my friends, long time no see," said GP.

"Only 24 years," laughed Alec.

After much hand shaking and introductions, the six headed off to the first tee. YGS had finished with Tiger and was waiting as they arrived.

"Gary," said AGS, "this is my son Gary."

"Pleased to meet you young man" said GP.

"Pleased to meet you too," said YGS, "I've heard so much about you from Dad, you've been an inspiration to him."

"That's very kind of you to say so Gary," said GP. He stole a glance at AGS and smiled.

"This man has inspired us all," said Ernie as he shook young Gary's hand.

The magnificent 7 headed out into the gloom. By the 6th there was quite a bit of mist around so they all agreed to have some fun on Hogan's Alley.

All 7 tee'd up and hit off trying to take Hogan's line from '53. Ernie and Nick walked ahead off the tee accompanied by YGS, who was desperate to tell them how Tiger was playing.

The three amigos and GP held back a little for a chat.

Walking along-side them was Ben, who was complementing them on their drives.

"You've been here since May?" enquired Alec.

"That's correct Alec" said Ben, "been havin' a lot of

fun makin' mischief with the tourists, but I'm here on official business this week.

'Committee' business (as he tapped his nose), the fun gets cranked up a notch or two for the Open. We gotta make sure the golf course chooses the right champion."

They all laughed.

As they walked along through the mist Ben had them in stitches as he recalled some of the mischief he'd created for unsuspecting golfers. Up ahead Ernie and Nick reckoned GP was telling Popeye jokes, YGS had no clue.

When they got to the green, YGS was giving Ernie a putting lesson, the old 4 strolled up.

"This guy's good." said Ernie. "Hold the finish, don't worry about the result, simple as that."

"The confidence of youth," said GP smiling at AGS, "he had a good coach."

The rest of the round drifted along in a sea of calm, occasional mischief occurred, but the quality of the shot-making was such as to negate the effect.

When they were done, GP and the amigos agreed to meet up during the week for food and chat.

****

One week later 18th fairway....

"So Ben," asked Bob, "the Frenchman has a 3 stroke

lead, what are you going to do?"

"Well Bob," said Ben, "he already thinks he's won, he's very nervous on the tee, look at the way he is moving around."

Jean van de Velde made his move. The ball sailed to the right as a defensive swing ensured the out of bounds left would be avoided. Fortune appeared to favour the Frenchman as his ball carried just over the Barry Burn to the right.

Recognising the lucky break for what it was, Jean thought the worst was over and he could comfortably carry the burn in front of the green make at worst a 5 and the jug would be his.

A 5-iron was selected. At the top of the backswing Ben whispered, "Don't hook" and Jean's body out raced his arms.

The result again was a push with the ball striking the grandstand before landing in deep rough.

"Nice one Ben," said Bob.

"Well Bob," said Ben, £there was a bit of arrogance in that club selection there. Remember in '68 when Gary laid up short of the burn knowing a five would probably be good enough for victory. That's the clarity of thought required in such circumstances."

****

There was to be no clarity of thought for Jean though, in what remained of his championship. The clarity and the Jug belonged to a young Scot from Aberdeen who birdied the last two holes of a four hole play-off. Paul Lawrie became the Champion Golfer of the year.

Back in the Caley Club the three amigos and YGS were enjoying the party.

"The golf course certainly chose Paul," said AGS, "what a finish"!

"AYE!" went the cry. Glasses were clinked, and the room rocked… All night long…

11

AUGUSTA GEORGIA APRIL 2007

"Welcome gentlemen" said chairman Bob, "to the 71st Masters Tournament and the 35th meeting of The Masters Mischief Making Committee."

Tapping of glasses and stamping of feet.

The committee now comprised 6 members, Bob Jones, Dwight Eisenhower, Jimmy Demaret, Sam Snead, Ben Hogan and Gene Sarazen.

"It's 4 years since Sam here joined us and in that time we've enjoyed unprecedented levels of mischief here at Augusta.

 He has made the 11th hole his cathedral of pain, for those who would treat her with disdain."

Chuckles.

"I'm delighted to announce here today, that we have a new member to welcome into our midst. Please be upstanding gentlemen, I give you Lord.. Byron.. Nelson"!! Roars and stamping of feet.

The doors swung open and in walked the third member of the American Triumvirate. All the members walked round to shake his hand, he beamed his Texas smile and took his seat between Jimmy and Ben.

"Byron" said Bob, "the committee are delighted to

THE FUNDAMENTAL TRUTH

welcome you to your first Masters as a mischief maker." Tapping of glasses.

"The first Order of Business gentlemen, as tradition dictates, is the review and approval of the qualification guidelines by which membership of this esteemed body of men may be achieved." Murmurs of agreement.

I use the term, 'body' loosely, given our appearance as it now stands. Byron here is looking very fresh as a recent arrival, but as we know gentlemen; copious amounts of malt whiskey consumption tends to have a detrimental effect on one's appearance.

Just look at Jimmy here, we haven't had a light on, even in our overnight meetings since his arrival, such is the strength of his whisky glow!" Tapping and laughing.

"Membership, of course, is by invitation only, and our guidelines which help us decide our invitees are as follows.
1) Has won a Grand Slam.
2) Has won 3 Masters Tournaments.
3) Has won at least 50 PGA tour events.
4) Has won a World War and is a former President of the U.S.A.

"Before I continue gentlemen, Dwight would like to say a few words."

"Thank you Bob," said Dwight, "good morning gentlemen and welcome Byron, we look forward to seeing your version of the Texas Twister, Ben and Jimmy's went down a storm when they came up with idea back in '04.

He cleared his throat "I believe that the time has come for guideline No.4 be removed from the list, as it is unlikely that it will be invoked in future."

Shallow murmurs around the room.

"I understand you reluctance gentlemen, as it is like, 'my rule', but the situation in North Korea and The Middle East not with-standing, the likelihood of another world war is remote to say the least."

Quiet chuckles ensued.

"Our current President is trying his hardest to start a World War, his desire to join this esteemed group knows no bounds, but thankfully, to date, he has been unsuccessful." Tapping and laughing.

"Ok Dwight, thanks for that, the committee will vote on this at the end of the meeting," said Bob.

"The second order of business is the induction of new members. As you know gentlemen Lord Byron here qualifies under guideline number 3, having won 52 PGA tour events." Roars and stamping of feet.

"This brings our committee strength up to 7, which is most welcome given the amount of mischief we have to get up to these days. The patrons are very demanding, what with social media and improved TV coverage, we have to be on top of our game."

Roars of agreement.

"It pleases me no end to welcome another son of Texas to our group. I believe that leaves Gene here outnumbered 6 to 1, he'll be starting to get a complex!"

Much laughter and stamping of feet.

THE FUNDAMENTAL TRUTH

"If I may Mr Chairman," said Gene, "whilst I'm outnumbered 6 to 1, my mischief on 15 is 6 times as good as anyone else's." He displayed a broad smile.

"Ah yes Gene," said Bob, "modest as ever, you can take the man out of New York, but…" Another broad smile and more laughter.

"Ok gentlemen, to business," said Bob, "Myself and Dwight as always will have a roving commission, to make mischief all over the golf course, the clubhouse and particularly the TV compound."

Lord Byron here as a rookie will be given the par 3 tournament to, 'cut his teeth' as it were. On Thursday, if all goes well, Byron will take up residence on hole 13." Byron nodded and smiled.

"Ben, if you're agreeable, will resume your duties on no.12." Ben nodded and smiled.

"Sam, if you're agreeable, will resume duties on no.11." Sam nodded and smiled.

"Jimmy, if you're agreeable, will resume duties on no.16."

Jimmy nodded and sang, "Sweet 16, where I'm never seen, can be so mean, just after Gene, makes 'em wanna scream!! Sweet 16."

Laughter all round.

"Ok gentlemen thanks for that. Byron, as your in charge of the par 3 tournament on Wednesday, the tradition is that any qualified players who have not yet joined us are given a particularly warm reception, so don't go easy on them, they need to be prepared for the day they join us." Tapping and stamping.

"Any other business gentlemen?" asked Bob.

"If I may Mr. Chairman" said Ben," I note the Open is back at Carnoustie this summer and I would like to go over a couple of months early, I love it over there and I'm learning all new kinds of mischief which I'm sure will be of benefit to this committee."

"Very good Ben" said Bob, "any objections?" None were forthcoming. "Very well Ben, we look forward to your report next year."

"Ok gentlemen, can we now vote on the retention of guideline no. 4?"
A unanimous "AYE" went up. "Thank you gentlemen, as normal guideline no 4 is retained." Much laughter and stamping of feet.

"That concludes the formalities, Byron, if you will, please select one of our fine Speyside Malts in order that the informalities may commence."

And he did.

12

ARBROATH JULY 2007

The times they were a changing. The new first minister for Scotland, Alec Cargill thought as much as he looked out over the Firth of Tay from his upstairs lounge at Piesiehill Farm just to the west of the town.

The Farm owner, Brian Souter was a long-time friend of Alec and a cousin of Ian. He had never felt comfortable living in the big old sandstone farmhouse since his Mum and Dad passed on.

He was happy to sell the old house provided he could still own and run the farm. The cottage in the grounds was far more suited to his needs. Alec was delighted with his acquisition and wasted no time in converting the upstairs into a lounge with panoramic views across to Fife.

Sitting across from him enjoying some good Arbroath hospitality (Aberdeen Angus steaks and Arbroath Smokie) was an American businessman, Donald Trump, who was interested in expanding his golf course empire in Scotland.

Donald loved golf and was an accomplished player, his drive to create great new golf courses around the world new no limits.

The New Yorker recognised the world wide explosion in the game was a huge business opportunity, but he did insist that the courses he would create would impact on everyone who played them.

He wanted real estate that would encourage a

continued expansion of the game. Land where the environment benefited from the activity. Land where economies would grow in the surrounding areas.

His vision saw golf as the main pastime for all humanity.

"So Donald," said Alec, "fancy a game of golf tomorrow? Us Carnoustie members have courtesy of a number of Angus courses this week."

"Sure Alec," said Donald, "I hear Panmure next to Carnoustie is pretty good, how about there?"

"No problem Donald, I'll get my team right on it."

Alec's team, Ian Beattie and Gary Shepherd, at 64 were now retired from their careers in the fishing and oil industries but were persuaded by their good friend Alec that they could help him in his role as First Minister.

Ian had become Alec's chief advisor on Agriculture and Fisheries, while Gary filled a similar role on Energy, particularly renewables.

As the Scottish Parliament was in summer recess, the pair were carrying out their other duty as golfing partners for their good friend.

"That was Alec," said Ian putting the phone down, "he wants us to arrange a four-ball tomorrow at Barry, Donald Trump will make up the four."

"I hear he's quite a good player, off 6 or something," said Gary.

"Barry's just been used for Open qualifying so should

be in good nick," said Ian.

"Do you think Ben will be there?" asked Gary.

"I would imagine so." said Ian. "It's just over the railway from his summer residence and as you know, Ben misses nothing. He keeps up with all the political gossip and will be fully aware of Mr Trump's ambitions."

"Should be fun watching Ben 'interact' with Mr Trump," laughed Gary.

"Absolutely," laughed Ian, "American mischief incorporated."

Next morning at 11.00 a.m. the four arrived at the practice range.

"Gee guys," said Donald, "you take this seriously, we don't tee off till 12! I normally take 5 practice swings before hitting off."

"We learned from the best," said Alec, "Ben Hogan told us never to arrive at the first tee under-prepared."

"You knew Ben Hogan?!" said Donald astonished.

"We sure did," said Gary in his best Texan drawl.

For the first time in a long, long time, Donald Trump was speechless.

The warm up commenced in the time honoured fashion with Donald doing more watching than swinging.

"You guys hit it pretty good," he eventually pronounced, "don't tell me, you learned from Hogan."

"Correct," said Ian, "more specifically from the book, Hogan's 5 lessons – 'The Modern Fundamentals of Golf'."

"I think I read that once," said Donald, "but I didn't really study it. I've been kinda busy running my business empire."

"You should study it," said Alec. "It may help you in business and many other aspects of life."

"I will," said Donald and off they went to the first tee.

The match commenced on time with Donald partnering Alec against Ian and Gary. Four ball better ball was the match of choice with Donald receiving 5 strokes off the three scratch players.

The first 4 holes were halved and as they stood on the 5th tee Ian and Gary could see Ben strolling a few yards behind. Alec was aware as well so decided to introduce the business angle into the conversation.

"I really don't see a problem with your proposals for the development of a golf course and hotel complex on the Buddon peninsula Donald." He looked over at Donald.

"Defence spending in the UK. is being cut dramatically, the M.O.D. has many areas of land that would be suitable for a live firing range."

The players teed off, Alec and Donald walked of ahead while Ian and Gary hung back to talk to Ben.

"Hello old friend," said Ian, "how long have you been over?"

THE FUNDAMENTAL TRUTH

Ben smiled a warm smile. "Oh I guess about 8 weeks, the Masters Committee thought it would be a good idea to come early and get some mischief in."

Meanwhile, up ahead, business discussions continued.

"This golf course will be the best in the world," said Donald," I think that piece of real estate with the massive sand dunes overlooking St. Andrews will provide a test the will one day host The Open." He readjusted his cap. "The great infrastructure, roads, railway and an on-site Airfield make the overall package very attractive."

"I agree," said Alec, "and the boost to the Scottish economy will be significant. Tourism is becoming more important now that the oil is running out."

"These two up ahead look to be getting along great." said Ben, "I sure hope the project goes ahead. All that shootin' and hollerin' goin' on every day disturbs my mischief makin, not to mention my siesta."

They all laughed.

"So Ben," said Gary, "who do you think the golf course will choose next week?"

"I know Tiger is goin' for 3 in a row but I think he's lost his way since his father passed. He won last year shortly after Earl's death as he felt he was walking with him. I don't think he feels that anymore."

He adjusted his cap.

"I think it maybe a first time winner, the course is better set up than in '99, the weather looks to be pretty mixed, Carnoustie is in charge, with a little help from us of course."

When the four arrived at their tee shots, Donald was furthest away and made a pretty good pass at the ball.

"He's learning from you three," said Ben, "imitation is the best form of flattery, especially in golf."

The match continued in the same vein, the shot-making getting better and better.

"I can't remember ever playing this well," said Donald.

"You're starting to make a better move," said Alec, "you're instinctively copying what Ian, Gary and I are doing. You're moving to another level."

"I need to play with you guys more often," laughed Donald. "When can you come over to the States?"

"Maybe sooner than you think," said Alec. "We're heading to New York next month for a Climate Change Conference."

"That's great guys" said Donald, "look me up when you get there, I'll fix us up with a couple of games."

The match continued at a very high standard before concluding in a diplomatic half. No egos were bruised and business prospects were certainly enhanced.

"Will you be staying for the Open?" asked Ian.

"I'd love to," said Donald, "but I have a meeting with Rudi that I can't afford to miss, maybe next time."

THE FUNDAMENTAL TRUTH

With that they bade farewell.

****

Ben was waiting by the green and the amigos wandered over.

"I liked what Donald was proposing for the Buddon Peninsula," said Ben, "especially The Hogan Heritage Centre, I could get very excited about that, maybe create some indoor mischief."

"You could move in there permanently," laughed Gary, "a lot more comfortable than sleeping by the 6th tee."

"True" said Ben, "the gulls wake me up with their screaming at 4.00am every morning, the lack of sleep is playing havoc with my concentration."

They all laughed.

"Donald told me he'd already been in touch with the Ministry of Defence and a price has been agreed in principal. I'm sure our Parliament will be happy to sanction the new project as it will be a huge boost to the local economy."

"When do you think it will happen?" asked Ben.

"That, my friend, is the 64 dollar question. The amount of red tape that must be rolled out in this country, before any project can go ahead, has to be seen to be believed, ask me that question again in 5 years," laughed Ian.

They agreed to catch up at the end of the week, after the new champion was crowned…..

The amigos headed back to the Caley Club for a beer.

"So," said Alec, "what did you make of that?"
"He's some piece of work, is our Donald, he's certainly got ee's troosers on" laughed Ian.

"When did you find out about this, 'Buddon Project'?"

"Donald phoned me a couple of weeks ago. He said he was coming over to the, 'Old Country', his ancestral home, I believe. He loves his golf and sees opportunities all over the world with the growth of the game. He wants to leave his mark in Scotland."

"Did he tell you how much he's paying for the land?" asked Gary.

"No, but you can bet he negotiated a good deal, the pressure on defence spending is huge, now that the U.K's need to patrol the far corners of the globe has diminished."

Ben seemed happy with the prospect of more mischief opportunities, who knows, it may even become an Open venue in the future. I know Donald would love that."

Just then the door of the lounge swung open and in walked Gary Player. Now in his 70's Gary was no longer eligible to play in the Open. He didn't attend every year now but he knew he had to be at Carnoustie.
"Hello my friends," he piped up as he strolled over to their table, warm handshakes and hugs were exchanged before he sat among them.

"Ben's here," said Alec, "spoke with him this morning over at the Panmure Course."

"He's been here since May. He'd like to make it his permanent summer residence," said Ian, "Only go to Texas and Augusta over the winter months."

"How wonderful," said GP. "I take it he's still out by the 6th tee?"

"Yes," said Ian, "although developments this morning have got him all excited about a possible move."

"Do tell," said GP.

Donald Trump's plans were laid out in detail by the Three Amigos, GP listened intently without interruption, until they were finished.

"I love the sound of, "The Hogan Heritage Centre," said GP, "especially the coaching centre, when do you think it could be up and running?"

The three looked at each other and then back at GP.

"The land hasn't been bought yet," said Alec, "and there will be some obstacles put in our way that we don't even know about."

"I thought you fellows were in charge of Scotland now, quick work on that by the way, last time we met you were just a rookie MSP." said GP. "How did you manage that?"

"Right place at the right time," said Alec. "The main parties at Holyrood couldn't agree on a leader so I was the compromise candidate, my views and policies are well known and were acceptable to all sides."

He gestured sideways. "These two smilers either side of me are my, 'Special Advisors' they don't take a salary from the public purse, they seek rewards in other ways, if you know what I mean, nudge, nudge."

"I do I do," laughed GP. "So what are your plans for this great country over the next 5 years?"

"We want to enhance our position as the number one golfing destination in the world. Our golf courses are suffering due to climate change, our weather here in Scotland is becoming more unsettled, just look out the window, the lush fairways of Carnoustie today bear no resemblance to the yellow brown texture of previous decades."

"Is that not due to the on course watering?" asked GP.

"Partly," said Ian, "improvements in golf course management have created more consistent playing conditions and there is no doubt that tourists prefer to see grass under their ball before they swing, it's debateable if the on course watering is needed at all given the amount of rain we now seem to be getting."

"Beyond tourism, the country is not what it was Gary," said Alec, "the heavy industries of the past are no more, we are only a small population, our temperate climate allows us to have the best food production, in terms of quality.

We export vast amounts of produce, but the former heavy industrial areas are still in decline. We used to have the best education system in the world, and we need to get back up there if we are to grasp the opportunities that the new high tech industries will create. We can't have every one making whisky, hee-hee."

"Good speech boss," said AGS, "now, more important

THE FUNDAMENTAL TRUTH

matters, who's going to lift the Claret Jug on Sunday?"

"I've got a name for you from my native South Africa," said GP, "a young man who has 'the move' well grooved, Louis Oosthuizen."

"What about your mate Ernie?" asked AGS.

"Ernie's always got a chance," said GP, "but I think his putting's gone back a little and Carnoustie doesn't quite fit his eye."

"What do you mean, 'quite fit his eye'? The golf course covers over 100 acres, it won't fit any ones eye," laughed AGS.

"I hear that term used a lot over in the States," laughed GP.

"I don't know what it means either, I assume it means 'I don't think I can win, but I'll turn up and make a lot of money anyway'."

"Where and when can we meet next week?" asked Alec.

"Caley Club Sunday evening," said Ian, "remember the party in '99."

"No," said AGS,"I have no recollection of that event."

They all laughed at the memory.

****

Sunday afternoon 18th fairway.

Ben had been tasked with making mischief on 17 and 18 as had been the case in '99.

Sergio Garcia had led The Open from Thursday after an opening round of 65. As the leaders approached the finishing holes it was clear that the winner would come from one of three players. Garcia, Romero and Harrington.

"Who do you like Ben?" asked Bobby Jones.

"To be honest with you Bob I think Sergio follows my teachings the closest and has played the best golf. Romero has come out of nowhere but I don't think he's ready for the enormity of the task facing him. Harrington has come back from 6 behind and he's paid his dues on the range.

My good friend Bob Torrance has dedicated his life following my principals, his son Sam whilst being very talented hasn't shown the same discipline.

I think the golf course will choose the Irishman, Bob will be very happy."

13

NEW YORK AUGUST 2008

"Welcome gentlemen," said Donald, "to my humble abode."

Trump Tower in Manhattan was anything but humble. It was a demonstration of Donald Trump's success. The 3 amigos strolled around the panoramic lounge looking over the night time skyline, the sounds of the city far below.

"Thanks for the invitation Donald," said Alec, "It's our first time in New York City and it's a world away from Arbroath."

"Yes it is," said Donald," but the people are not so different, there's a lot of us here and we've had to build upwards to accommodate everyone, but fundamentally we work hard and play hard just like you guys."

"I think you're right Donald," said Ian, "people who come to New York are risk takers, they're prepared to suffer to achieve they're dreams. The dreams are different in Arbroath, but they mean the same to the people there."

"When does your climate change conference start?" asked Donald.

"Day after tomorrow," said Alec, "gives us a free day for relaxing and seeing the sites."

"Ok," said Donald, "let's leave the golf till next week once your business is concluded, I don't want to take advantage of your jet lag, I've studied the book and my game's looking better than ever."

"We'll be the judge of that," laughed Gary.

"I've placed a limo at your disposal for tomorrow, the driver will take you wherever you want to go, just don't ask him to show you the sites. The sites he'll want to show you ain't on any tourist map."

"I like the sound of that." laughed Gary, "The real New York, as long as we don't go to Yankee Stadium, I'll be happy."

"What, are you a Red Sox fan Gary?"

"We all are," said Alec. "Remember that night in the Bronx when Curt Schilling pitched with blood seeping out of his ankle? We were glued to the TV. The whisky flowed that night I can tell you."

"That's OK guys, I'm a Mets fan. I hate the Yankees too."

Next morning the Amigos were picked up and headed out into the city. The air was sticky hot and Marvin, the driver, had the air con working at full tilt.

"Morning gentleman, welcome to New York City, my name is Marvin and I will be your guide for today."

"Thank you Marvin I'm Alec and this is Ian and Gary it's our first time in New York. We've been awake since 2a.m. already been down to Grand Central Station, Empire State and Times Square. Came back up to the Tower for breakfast, then had a stroll round Central Park."

Marvin laughed, "You guys will fit right in here. This is

the city that never sleeps. Would you like me to show you the sites?"

"You bet," said Gary as the others gave him a look.

And he did.

Next morning the Amigos were taken to the conference at the UN building feeling more than a little jet lagged.

The first three speakers droned on about the crisis facing the planet, and the need to cut carbon emissions. The latest buzz words being carbon footprint. This term was now seen as the best indicator, and easiest way to measure the effect of greenhouse gases on the planet's climate.

"How are you coping?" asked Alec of Gary who was slumped in his seat.

"Just about keeping awake, we certainly saw the sights yesterday. Maybe my idea was a little hasty knowing we were coming here today."

"You could say," laughed Ian, "Marvin certainly showed us around the sights."
"Don't remind me," said Gary. "New York unplugged I think he called it, I'm struggling to switch off."

"This conference will help you," said Alec. "It's the same old, same old. We're all struggling to keep awake."

Next day the conference had moved on to possible solutions to the climate change issue. Scientists from all over presented their ideas which were varied in the extreme.

There was one, however, which fired the Amigo's interest.

They knew they had to meet with the young Californian.

And they did.

14

AUGUSTA GEORGIA APRIL 2017

Chairman Bob Jones welcomed the members of the Masters Mischief Making Committee to the annual jamboree otherwise known as 'The Masters Tournament. The committee still comprised the magnificent 7 who had been making mischief as a group since 2007. That was about to change.

"First order of business gentlemen is to inform you that we have a new inductee to welcome to our midst. Please be upstanding as we welcome, Arnold, 'The King' Palmer!"

Loud roars and stamping of feet.

The doors to the lounge swung open and in strode the man himself smiling from ear to ear. Warm handshakes and back slapping ensued as people recoiled from the famous Palmer grip. In this environment, however the pain was more like a tickle, the members were recoiling at the thought of the old grip which in many cases required a week's physio to recover from.

"Thank you Bob," said Arnold as he moved to his place at the table.

"In time honoured fashion," said Bob, "the next order of business is to re-state the qualification guidelines by which membership of this esteemed body maybe gained.
1)   Has won a Grand Slam.
2)   Has won 3 Masters Tournaments
3)   Has won at least 50 PGA tour events.

4)   Has won a world war and is a former President of the U.S.A.

Before I continue gentlemen, Dwight would like to say a few words."

"Morning gentlemen" said Dwight, "and may I say it's a matter of personal delight to see Arnold here take his seat beside us." Here here's and tapping of glasses.

"I know that I'm prone to drone, with regard to the 'guidelines' but I really do feel that it is time to remove guideline no 4 from the list as it is unlikely that it will ever be invoked in the future."

"I understand your reticence in removing this for nostalgic reasons, with me being a founding member of this committee.

"The situation in North Korea and the Middle East not with-standing, the likely-hood of another world war is remote to say the least."

Murmurs around the room

Our new President Donald Trump has so far adopted a softly-softly approach to the hotspots of the world and it has to be said that this committee had no little influence in getting him elected. Be careful what you wish for, even as Republicans."

Silence.

"This committee must remain vigilant if we are to maintain the status quo."

"Ok Dwight, thanks for that, the committee will vote

THE FUNDAMENTAL TRUTH

on this at the end of our meeting" said Bob.

"Back to the induction gentlemen. As we know Arnold here qualifies through his four Masters wins and his 62 PGA tour titles."

Applause and stamping of feet.

"This brings our committee strength up to 8 which is most welcome given the amount of mischief we're now required to produce."

Stamps and giggles. Somewhere in the room a chair toppled over.

"Arnold's arrival will certainly improve the quality if his swashbuckling style of play is transferred to mischief making."

Tapping of glasses.

"As normal, Arnold as a rookie, will be put in charge of mischief at the par 3 tournament on Wednesday. On Thursday, if all goes well, Arnold will take up residence on 18, he feels it owes him."

Much laughter.

"Before we allocate the holes for this year, I think it's appropriate to mention the outstanding mischief performed by Ben on hole 12 last year. Ben if you would."

"Thank you Bob for these kind words. Last year, though I say so myself, was a moment of personal triumph and my most effective mischief making … so far."

Laughing and tapping.

"If I may, I'd like to take you back to the Sunday afternoon and my position on the bridge at the 12th hole. Young Texan Jordan Spieth had arrived on the tee having just dropped a shot on 11. I'd spoken to Sam and he agreed to soften him up with a clumsy bogey."

Whistles ensued.

"Jordan was still well in the lead and looking like he would have a comfortable run in to retain his green jacket. I could see that Jordan was ripe for mischief as he debated for too long on club and shot selection. I was sitting on my bridge doing my usual with the wind, keeping it fairly steady into, until the players addressed the ball."

He paused for dramatic effect.

"The patrons of course, in their thousands, assist with the usual sharp intake of breath, as the tension mounts. Increasing the velocity. They then hold their breath as one, when the backswing commences. This creates an impression of no wind at the top of the backswing and the player panics thinking they have too much club. Too late!! They take a little off the shot to compensate. A watery grave usually awaits…"

Groans of agreement.

"Jordan was in shock, the patrons gasped as one and were still muttering as Jordan, all too quickly, decided where to drop. His heart was pounding, his colour was draining from his face. He hardly made it to the ball with his next swing."

A pin could have dropped in the room at this point.

The gasps got louder as the second ball ended in Rae's Creek. He did well to make a 7 after that. Jordan's a fine young Texan, and a credit to the game. He now knows we don't like processions here at Augusta."

Much applause and stamping of feet.

"Thank you Ben" said Bob, "outstanding work.

Ben took his seat.

"Ok gentlemen, to business. Dwight and I, as always, will have a roving commission to make mischief all over the golf course, the clubhouse and particularly, the TV compound."

Tapping on tables.

"Some of you may have noticed Dwight is spending more and more time out on 17, at the spot where 'his tree' used to stand. The tree, as we know was cut down in '02 after being damaged in an ice storm. At least that's the, 'official story'. We know it better as an IKE storm." Chuckles all around.

"The unofficial version saw Dwight get in touch with a local tree surgeon, who owed him a favour, pleasantries were exchanged, but the surgeon was left in no doubt what was expected of him. After the tree's removal, which Dwight witnessed, he regretted immediately, his decision. He'd seen enough death in his life, the tree's death was as a result of his loss of composure on the golf course.

He paused.

"He now stands on that spot for hours; it helps him deal with all the lives that were lost under his command."

Nods of acknowledgement. Dwight was staring into the distance.

"Sam, Ben, Byron, Gene and Jimmy, I take it your happy to resume duties on last year's hole allocations.?" Nods of approval.

"Very well gentlemen" said Bob, "before putting the retention of guideline 4 to the vote, we have a visitor from overseas coming to join us for this year's mischief making."

A few sat up in their chairs.

All the way from Spain…please welcome Severiano Ballesteros!"

Loud roars and stamping of feet.

"Hola mi Amigos," said Seve as he strode into the room. "It's great to be back!"

More roars and stamping.

"I have to say I am very honoured to have been asked by the Open Mischief Makers Committee to be the first non-Masters member to visit Augusta. Although I do have a couple of green jacket's tucked away in Padrena."

Bob wasn't laughing.

"Gene's mischief in '86 was beautiful. I've learned a lot of things at the Open, working alongside Ben, Bob and Gene here. These three gentlemen see the exchanges between our committees as essential to the continued improvement of our product.

THE FUNDAMENTAL TRUTH

Both committees have been innovative in their development of new talent, myself being a perfect example. My 'Miracle at Medinah' was a direct result of their coaching. Always expect the unexpected gentlemen."

Much laughter.

"The Ryder Cup offers the best opportunity for mischief making in Golf, mainly due to the extra pressure associated with the event. Arnold here got an unexpected opportunity at Hazeltine last year. That was great work with the bag on the first tee Arnold, pure theatre."

"Why thank you Seve," said Arnold, "I was inspired by the symbol of your clenched fist pose sewn on the shirts of the Europeans. They felt you were walking with them."

"I was," laughed Seve, "or should I say I was sitting in Ollie's buggy, buzzing all over the place, reminded me of Valderrama in '97.

I was the ultimate back street drive. It's a miracle Ollie didn't end up in hospital!" Much laughter.

"I'm grateful for this opportunity to make mischief at the Masters, as I'm sure Arnold will be when he sits by his plaque at Birkdale in July." Much Applause.

"Ok Seve, thanks for that," said Bob, "all that remains of official business is the vote. All those in favour of retaining guideline 4 say aye.

"AYE," went the shout. Dwight shook his head.

"Very well gentlemen, Dwight here will continue to monitor the World War situation on a year to year basis."

Cheers and Stamping of feet.

"Arnold, if you would be so kind, please select one of our fine Speyside malts, in order that the informalities may commence."

"My pleasure" said Arnold as he selected a 12 year old Balvenie double wood.

****

Sunday afternoon 15th hole.

Seve is standing alongside Gene. Bob and Dwight are close by.

"So my friend," said Seve. "Tell me about the shot that was, "heard around the world."

"Well Seve," said Gene "as you know, this was only the second Masters Tournament and at that time there was no Mischief Making Committee in place."

Bob here was still playing and Dwight was playing soldier in some far off place. I felt that the golf course wanted me to go for that shot, not lay-up.

When I hit it, man it was a thing of beauty, not so high, it's flight was framed against the trees at the back of the green.

When it landed, I got such a jolt of adrenalin, like I'd never felt before, pure electricity coursing through my veins. I somehow knew it was going to go in." Bob and Dwight were listening in…

Meanwhile on the fairway, Sergio swung on pure

adrenalin with an 8 iron that soared with a real purpose towards the flag in the middle of the green. Seve glanced round and knew his mischief was working.

"When that little darlin' rolled up, kissed the pin and fell in, well I don't mind tellin you fellas, I wanted to run across the water so euphoric was I" said Gene.

"Thankfully my caddie reminded me that soggy tweeds at Augusta are a definite no no"! Laughter all around.

"I floated home after that to claim the Tournament. The golf course certainly chose me back in '35."

A huge roar erupted from around the 15th green. Sergio had holed his eagle putt. They all looked at Seve who shrugged. Laughter ensued.

As Sergio moved to the 16th tee, he was now in the hands of Jimmy D, who sang.
"Sweet 16 belongs to me, you take your club, you place your tee, you make your swing, so nice and free, but sweet 16 belongs to me."

Seve intervened.

"Hey Jimmy, great outfit man," He said.

"The Wardrobe," was today dressed in Arnold's rainbow colours, in honour of the new member from Latrobe.

"Thanks Seve," said JD,"I always try to dress appropriately for the occasion."

"Green hat, red shirt, blue trousers and white shoes?" joked Seve.

"Yep I was particularly keen, whilst honouring Arnold, not to forget about Tiger, who couldn't be with us this week."

"Nice touch," said Seve.

Meanwhile, the roar behind them confirmed that Sergio's ball had come to rest a mere 5ft behind the hole.

Jimmy D turned, looked back at Seve, winked "Sweet 16 belongs to me" he sang. Sergio missed the putt.

On 17, Dwight was standing to the left of the fairway with his arms stretched out. He actually looked like a tree. Bob was trying to calm him down.

Ben took over.

Sergio swung on the tee, he remembered the move. He'd had it all his life.

Ben smiled as the ball took off down the left side of the fairway. Dwight's arms flailed as he tried to make a grab for it, then the fade took hold.

Ben walked the rest of the way with Sergio, he never missed a step.

Arnold was talking with Justin Rose's Dad up on 18, congratulating him on his fine work at Merion.

It was Sergio's time.

15

ROYAL BIRKDALE ENGLAND JULY 2017

(Meeting of The Open Mischief Makers Committee)

The committee room was a decent size, seating for 20, a bar and billiard table off to the side, perfect for post meeting entertainment.

The chairman, Old Tom Morris, stood to address the ensemble.

"Gentlemen" opened Tom. "It falls to me, as your Chairman, to open these proceedings in the time honoured fashion."

He leaped onto the billiard table with his trusty putter in hand and stroked three putts with the minimum of fuss, into the top left hand corner.
Loud cheering and stamping of feet.

Applause was impossible due to the hands being full of a malt whisky filled Quaich.

"Thank you gentlemen" said Tom. "I now declare the meeting open."

"First order of business, is to announce that no new prospective members have arrived on the scene.

As you know Seve here was our last inductee back in '12, appropriately, at the scene of his first Open victory at Lytham." Nods of acknowledgement.

"Seve, if you would, please present your report on your trail-blazing visit to Augusta in April. The committee are very keen to hear of your adventure across the pond."

Seve got to his feet.

"Thank you chairman Tom. As you know, Augusta has been running its own mischief since '73, when Dwight and Bob here formed a committee of two.
They adopted the same principals to mischief making as we have here, and have been very successful in creating some memorable moments.

I can attest to their effectiveness from personal experience." Laughing and tapping.

"I will always be grateful to the members here for allowing me the opportunity to visit a place that will always be dear to me, in an official capacity."

"I have to say my friends, that I was made most welcome by the Masters Committee and in particular, chairman Bob here who ensured I was given a free reign in my attempts to manage the mischief of Dwight." Laughing and tapping.

"And so to my report. Generally, I floated around the course over the first three days, creating the odd bit of mischief here and there, usually wind related."

"Not that I'm saying that Danny's Champions Dinner menu was responsible, but the Yorkshire pudding certainly worked my system." Chuckles.

"By Sunday I was pretty familiar with what was going on and enjoying my role in the fun. I was observing Sergio and Justin going head to head on the back nine and I sat down with Ben on his bridge." Ben nodded.

"I could tell that Ben was contemplating a different approach from the previous year so I asked him what he thought."

"Looks like Sam's having fun with Sergio, Justin's got the momentum now, " he said.

"What are you going to do?" I asked.

"I don't feel like interfering on this hole," he said, "Sergio needs a little recovery time, to make it interesting for the Patrons."

"Justin's too strong just now. I don't think my mischief would have any effect. I think his Dad is riding shotgun."

"Ben suggested we go speak with Byron on 13, see what he thought". Byron was full of mischief.

"Well hello gentlemen" he said with a twinkle in his eye.

"I see Sergio's struggling with the move Ben. That was some drive he hit off 11."

"The drive was solid." said Ben. "The starting line was a little too far left, the fade marginal. He got a straight first bounce, all Sam's doing of course. He hates anyone hitting fades on this golf course."

"I asked Byron what he thought Sergio would do on 13."

"This hole demands a draw," said Byron. "but I don't think Sergio can trust himself to execute the draw. I see him trying to hit a high fade off the left trees."

"The three of us looked back to the tee to watch Justin and Sergio tee off. Justin nailed a straight one, perfectly located. Sergio hit the same shot as 11, solid, but just not high enough. Byron made no mischief. The trees managed that on their own. I watch Sergio as he goes through the process of taking the penalty drop and preparing to hit his third shot. I could see the tension leaving his body. He was giving up control to gain control. The tension was switching to Justin, it looked likely he was going to have at least a three shot lead standing on the 14th tee. It was now his Masters, to lose…"

He paused

"I have to say, I was starting to get excited for Sergio when he matched Justin's 5 on 13, I sensed the only mischief I would have to make, was to minimise the effect of Gene, Jimmy D and Dwight. I think I did a pretty good job."

Tapping and laughing.

"I felt that both Ben and Bob were happy to let Sergio play free for The Masters." Both men nodded and smiled.

"Sergio proved worthy of their faith. The freer we are gentlemen, the richer the experience. Muchas gracias."

"Thank you Seve," said Old Tom, "for your thorough and entertaining report. I have to say, Augusta sounds like a very beautiful and exiting place."

He shuffled the papers before him. "Let me just check,

THE FUNDAMENTAL TRUTH

ah yes, I believe only 7 of our 15 members have visited Augusta. Seve of course, Ben, Bob, Gene, Walter, Henry and of course Mr Locke."

He looked over to Bob.

"I was wondering Bob, would it be possible to arrange a visit for the entire committee next year, purely as observers you understand, we wouldn't interfere with any of your wonderful production, unless asked to assist of course."

"Certainly," said Bob. "Should have done it years ago, give the committee a chance to sample some good ol' southern hospitality."

"Thank you Bob." said Tom. "We would of course, reciprocate at next year's Open at Carnoustie."

"Thank you Tom," said Bob. "I know Jimmy D would love to team up with Ben at the scene of his Open victory. Every year at Augusta, Ben recounts his love of Scotland, the people, the golf courses, the whisky. Jimmy will be salivating severely at the prospect."

"Talking of welcoming guests," said Tom, "please show your appreciation in the usual manner for a special guest all the way from Latrobe, Pennsylvania: Mister... Arnold... Palmer..."!

Roars and stamping as the doors swung open revealing, "The King" in all his glory.

Everyone stood to welcome Arnold individually, shaking his hand. Arnold was impressed by the strength of the grips of the Old timers. There was no wincing here. He strode to his allotted place.

I. A. SHEPHERD

"Thank you Mr. Chairman," said Arnold. "I am so honoured and humbled to be invited back to Birkdale, the scene of my first Open victory."

Tapping of quaichs .

"Looking around this table, I see many faces I know, and many I know only from the history books, where the record of their great achievements, in golf and life, are numerous and full." More tapping.

"When I first started playing golf, my father told me,"Son, whatever you go on to achieve in golf, and in life, make sure you stay true to your spirit, play free and live free. I see that I am among kindred spirits here." More tapping and stamping.

"Thank you Arnold," said Tom, "please do grab a seat." The King settled in a wide armchair in the corner.

The second order of business today gentlemen, is the allocation of holes.

Tradition dictates that committee members who have won an Open at the venue of the day, have first choice. Although not a committee member, Arnold here is the only previous winner at Birkdale.

As our honoured guest, Arnold, we would be delighted if you would do us the honour of making your own special brand of mischief, at a hole of your choice."

"Why thank you Mr. Chairman," said Arnold, "I would be delighted."

"Including Arnold, therefore, I believe our numbers for

this year's mischief, have swelled to 16. This puts us in the envious position of being able to cover all the holes comfortably, especially if our Grand Slam winners continue the tradition of taking two holes each.

Prestwick winners like myself, young Tom here and Willie Park look forward to getting the left overs as normal." Chuckles.

"Don't know what you're laughing at Gene, you won at Princes." More chuckles.

"As I understand it, only one of us has victories at more than three current venues, that would be Bobby, 'Old Baggy Pants' Locke." Tapping of Quaichs.

"On the subject of current venues, does anyone know if Turnberry, or should I say President Trump Turnberry is still on the rota?"

"The R&A have announced venues, only till 2020 Mr Chairman," said Henry. "Carnoustie, Royal Portrush and Royal St. Georges."

"Thank you Henry," said Old Tom, "well, we can be sure to be sure, that none of us has won there before." Chuckles.

"First time venue, Portrush I believe, in Northern Ireland, no less."

"They have their own mischief makers over there, don't they?" asked Walter, "called leper cons or something." Hilarity.

"That would be Leprechauns Walter." said Baggy Pants. "Fred Daly told me all about them, said they looked a bit like Gene... but with a beard." More hilarity.

"That's good intel Bobby," said Old Tom. "We'll need to discuss this further at next year's meeting, we can't have two sets of mischief makers causing havoc, the winning score would be over 320"!! Yet more hilarity.

"So Arnold," said Tom, "would you care to choose a hole at which you would like to commence your mischief making?"

All eyes turned towards, "The King."

"Well Mr. Chairman," he said, "I guess everyone expects me to choose no.15, as it's the site of my famous bush recovery shot, but if you don't mind, I'd like to take up residence on hole no.13, not that I'm superstitious you understand." Much laughter.

"I feel that hole 13 on the final round is the place where you can set yourself free and still claim the prize. The first 12 holes are more like a game of chess, moves are tried, nerves are raw, more moves, changes of strategy. By 13 the end game can be seen, look at Sergio at this year's Masters, no.13 set him free. As you know, that's how I like to play the game, charging to the finish with all guns blazin', hee-hee." Nods of Approval.

"Any objections gentlemen?" asked Old Tom. "No? Very well then, LET THE BIDDING COMMENCE"! Chaos.

After half an hour the members slowly returned to their seats, some smiling, some frowning. The horse trading was more severe than normal. Maybe it was Arnold's mention of freedom got the members a little excited.

"Ok gentlemen let's say no more about hole allocations today, anyone who is not satisfied with their position may, if they wish, make it an item for discussion at next year's meeting." Nods of approval.

"That concludes the formalities gentlemen. Arnold, if you would, please select one of our fine Speyside malts in order that the informalities may commence."

"My pleasure" said Arnold as he selected a 15 year old Macallan. The cheers resounded.

Sunday afternoon 13th hole.

"So Bob," said Arnold, "it looks to me as though you've been having fun with Jordan there."

Jordan Spieth was standing on the tee preparing to hit. Bob was standing alongside all the early hole mischief makers, who were looking very pleased with themselves.

"We felt that Jordan needed to be tested again after what occurred at Augusta this year. He was still thinking about what happened to him in '16 over the course of the final round, and it took a little off his performance."

"Well he's still thinking about it now," laughed Arnold, as he watched Jordan swing on the tee, and hold his head in his hands.

Arnold moved quickly, faster than a speeding bullet.

He tapped one of the spectators on the shoulder, who turned and caught a glimpse of Jordan's ball plummeting into the side of a massive sand dune, over 100 yards away from the middle of the 13th fairway. Without Arnold's mischief, there was little doubt that the ball would have been declared lost.

Jordan strolled dejectedly over to where the ball was. He climbed to the top of the dune to assess the situation. The physical effort got his heart pumping for a different, better reason.

He knew he'd been lucky to find the ball, he climbed back down. This was no Jean van de Veld at work here. When he got back to the ball he declared it unplayable.

The group of mischief makers were muttering among themselves, but were unanimous in their decision, not to interfere ... yet. Arnold was observing Jordan.

"Jordan's using the time well" he said to Bob, "by the time the officials tell him where to drop, he'll be free of worrying about losing, he'll be ready to attack and think about winning."

Bob agreed, "I think we'll keep out of Jordan's way, he'll have enough to worry about what Matt's doing."

"Should be fun," said Arnold, "I feel a charge coming on."

16

AUGUSTA GEORGIA APRIL 2018

(Meeting of The Masters Mischief Makers Committee)

"Welcome gentlemen" said Chairman Bob, "and an especially warm welcome to our dastardly dozen from across the pond." Much tapping of glasses and stamping of feet.

"I hope Jimmy D here is fulfilling his role as your host, to the best of his ability, which, I might add, is considerable.

Is the accommodation satisfactory? "Aye", came the unanimous shout.

"The accommodation is wonderful," said Henry, "and the nightly entertainment would wow Vegas, not that I've ever been there you understand." Hilarity.

"What happens in Vegas stays in Vegas huh Henry," laughed, "The Haig."

"I'd no idea what a wardrobe stripper was" laughed Henry, "until Jimmy started taking his clothes off, whilst singing 'I Walk The Line' and 'Fulsom Prison Blues'."

"Don't worry fellas," piped up Jimmy, "tonight.. for your entertainment... I'm gonna be..., 'The Rat Pack'. Roars of approval.

"I've got a medley lined up, ably assisted by Gene, 'The Mouse' Sarazen." More hilarity.

I. A. SHEPHERD

"You're no body till somebody loves you."

"Everybody 'aww'," said Gene.

"Me and my shadow."

"Yeah you love yourself Jimmy," said Gene.

"When your love has gone."

"Paranoia settling in," said Gene.

"What kind of fool am I"

"Delusional," said Gene.

"I'm gonna sit right down and write myself a letter."

"Delusional and illiterate," said Gene.

"Too marvellous for words."

"A delusional illiterate ego maniac," said Gene.

Much more hilarity.

"Ok Jimmy and Gene," said Bob, "I'm glad you're keeping our friends entertained." The noise calmed.

"The first order of business today is the review of our qualification guidelines. We have no new inductees to process and this year we have plenty of outside help. Should be a relaxing week. Let me restate for the record, our current list of guidelines."

1) Has won at least 3 Masters Tournaments.
2) Has won a Grand Slam.

3) Has won at least 50 PGA tour events.
4) Has won a world war and is a former President of the U.S.A.

"Before I continue gentlemen Dwight would like to say a few words."

"Morning gentlemen" said Dwight looking very serious, "after many month's monitoring the World War situation, I have to report that we are on the brink of winning… again."

Loud roars and stamping of feet.

"President Trump, with his ingenious use of twitter, is within days, if not hours of winning the Word War on Terror.
All over the world arms are being laid down as the Trump mantras are being followed religiously." Much stamping of feet and tapping of glasses.

"It should be obvious what this means to us all. By the 2021 Masters or at the latest 2025, former President Trump will be eligible for election to this committee." Hushed silence.

"If I may interrupt for a moment" said Ben, "this scenario has been anticipated for some time."

"With that in mind, I took the opportunity to ask our friends in Scotland, particularly former First Minister Alec Cargill to speak with his good friend and former business partner. Let me quote from his report."

"Donald and I discussed the situation over a few rounds of golf at the new 'Trumps Triumph' complex at Barry Buddon.

I. A. SHEPHERD

He was made aware of the Mischief Committees at both the Masters and the Open, but he thought it was just more fake news.

He says he has no interest in joining these two or any other of the thousands of committees, he's been asked to join when he retires." Stamping and tapping.

"He feels that with the power of twitter at his disposal, once he leaves the Oval Office, he will effectively become President of the World." Silence.

"I explained to Donald that membership of the Masters Mischief Making Committee, could only be achieved after death.

He thought about this for a few moments. He asked if this was a committee of ghosts.

I confirmed that the committee resides in another dimension, a sort of parallel universe. More, 'Fake News' he said."

"Ok Ben thanks for that," said Bob, "Ok gentlemen, given what we have just heard, can we vote on the removal of guideline 4?" A unanimous AYE went up.

"Thank you gentlemen, guideline 4 is hereby removed, Dwight here will be our only member so inducted." Loud cheers and stamping. A wide grin came over Dwight's face.

17

ARBROATH JULY 2018

"Are you sure you'll be able to caddy" asked Alec. "The R&A frown on trolleys being used in the Open, It's bad for the image."

"I'm not using a trolley." said AGS. "Gary's got a light pencil bag, I'm happy to carry that, if he needs waterproofs and brolly, we've got people in the crowd placed close by."

Young Gary Shepherd had qualified for the Open at the first attempt. Still an amateur and at 34 years of age had no ambitions to turn professional. He was happy earning a living at the Trump Triumph Resort at Barry Buddon.

He'd been trained as a Teacher, but decided a change of career was needed after he suffered the loss of his daughter Olivia back in 2010. She was only 14 months old and had died due to major heart defects.

The Trump project opened in 2012 and included The Hogan Heritage Centre. It was here that Gary gained employment as Hogan Historian, part time lecturer, part time guide, part time buyer of rare Hogan artefacts for exhibiting, and anything else that Ben asked him to do.

Ben was ever present, except from November through April, when he was State side. He, Young Gary and his Dad talked every day during the season. They were great friends.

Young Gary, dedicating himself to his work, as a result

had limited time to play the game. This year was different, however, with The Open being back at Carnoustie. Ben and his Dad persuaded him to enter. He had practised hard under Ben's supervision and qualified with three sub-par rounds.

"The weather forecast looks good for the week," said Ian, "so waterproofs shouldn't be necessary."

"This is Scotland Ian, not Spain." said Alec. "Remember, four seasons in one day."

"I know I'm 73," laughed Ian, "but that's something I wouldn't forget! The four seasons!" He broke into song with 'Walk Like A Man" and "Working my Way Back To You Girl".

"When is Young Gary going to Carnoustie to practice?" asked Alec.

"We're meeting Ben and GP tomorrow at 6.00am. Young Gary agrees that his first practice round should be on his own. We'll all be there advising on the strategy for winning at Carnoustie."

"Does Young Gary believe he can win?" asked Ian.

"Not at the moment," laughed AGS, "his target is to win the silver medal as low amateur."

"That's good," said Alec, "he has to build belief through actions."

6.00a.m. Tuesday morning 1st tee.

"I take it you've warmed up properly Gary," said Ben as he shook his hand.

THE FUNDAMENTAL TRUTH

"Of course Ben," said YGS. "Did my drills before breakfast."

"Change of plan." said Ben. "Mr. Player here is going to play with you. The R&A have changed the rules slightly. They now allow former Open Champions to play on the practice days, no matter what age they are."

YGS looked astounded.

"The public love it. Most only play a few holes, but Mr. Player here is not one of them."

"Shall we begin?" said GP as he teed his ball up. "I've been refining my move," as he looked from behind the ball to his target on the left side of the fairway.

YGS was observing closely. The ball took off low and straight, as it lost momentum, it started to fall to the right. Ben smiled.

Young Gary teed up, he was nervous of course, but he expected that. His pre-shot routine was identical to that of the 1968 champion. The result was the same. Ben smiled again.

As they walked across the Barry Burn, AGS, Alec and Ian dropped back a little.

"Talk about a clone!" exclaimed Ian. "I knew their swings were similar, but that was very strange seeing the two of them side by side."

"I see what you mean," said Alec. "They're of similar build. Young Gary's worked very hard on his physique, since he lost Olivia. He's as strong as GP now, so the move looks identical."

"GP's incredible," said Auld Gary."82 years young and still hitting the ball very well, look, their drives are out their side by side."

Up ahead the two Garys were striding purposefully towards their balls.

"Well Gary my friend," said GP, "so the adventure begins. How do you feel?"

"Pretty good Gary," said YGS."I was nervous on the first tee, but my move saw me through."

"Me too," laughed GP. It's been a while."

Hogan was walking briskly to the left of the fairway, watching everything, saying nothing.

They waited for the caddies to catch up.

"Come on auld man," laughed YGS,"I hope you can keep up, or this is going to be a long week, we don't want penalties for slow play."

"Don't worry son," said AGS, "these two auld yins here are a distraction, they'll be outside the ropes come Thursday."

The green on the first hole lay at an angle to the fairway, meaning the best approach to it was from the left side. Exactly where the two balls sat.

The distance to the pin was 172 yards. Shot options were varied, given the uphill lie and slight breeze from the west.

THE FUNDAMENTAL TRUTH

"Lie and wind add 15 yards to the 172?" asked GP of his caddy who confirmed.

GP asked for a 4 iron and he made his move. The ball took off as if in slow motion, climbing to 30ft max before falling off to the right, landing some 20ft from the pin.

"Shot," said YGS before selecting a 6 iron. He made his move, the ball climbed a little higher, but the result was the same. "Nice shot," said GP.

The rest of the round followed a similar pattern. Ben mostly observed but did step in with some advice to try different shot shapes from the same location, just to see how the ground treated them when they landed. YGS was receiving a golfing degree, in one morning.

Back in the Caley Club, the round analysis was well under way.

"I've got a lot more shots in my repertoire now," announced Young Gary.

"You certainly do," said Alec, "especially your ability to hit low fades, very useful if the wind gets up."

"I'm looking to you Dad, to help me choose the right one," said Young Gary.

"I've seen Carnoustie in all her moods son, we just have to recognise, which one she's in," said Auld Gary. "If we do, I'm sure we'll select the right ones."

"She seemed in a good mood today," said Ian. "The shots you and GP chose worked out pretty well."

"Ben made sure there wasn't any mischief going on

today," said Alec. "I think he and Bob would like to see an amateur do well this week, I think they like your chances Gary."

As Alec predicted, Young Gary's move continued to work beautifully over the next 5 days, he putted well, missing nothing inside 6ft, 3 putting only once, from 90 ft. on 14, but that was for a par.

By Sunday afternoon, he'd already secured the Silver Medal and was now setting his sights higher.

The Mischief Makers were up to their usual escapades. Dustin, Rory, Justin, Jordan, Jason, Ricky and the rest, were all getting a fair smattering of mischief, mainly due to their shot selection, which, unusually for them, was a little off.

Young Gary, meanwhile, was proceeding serenely along at
15 under par for the championship, which was 5 shots clear of the field. They were waiting on the 10th tee.

"The Haig" had been allocated the 10th. All the holes were covered comfortably this year with the visitors from across the pond being present.

20 Mischief Makers in total, all willing and able to cause mayhem. It was agreed at the pre-championship meeting, that Bob and Old Tom would have a roving commission, more like a Captain's role, although they were, theoretically at least, on the same side.

When the last group reached the 10th tee, potentially, there could be 12 Mischief Makers present on the one hole.

THE FUNDAMENTAL TRUTH

In practice, however, the "redundant" Mischief Makers tended to head for the beer tents and clubhouses, satisfied with their days work and relishing an opportunity to create a different type of mayhem.

The wind was off the sea, cool and grey conditions prevailed. Carnoustie was in the mood for a stern test, not unlike Jack and Gary faced, back in '68.

The preferred shape of shot on 10 in these conditions was a draw and,"The Haig" knew this. He also knew that Young Gary would not attempt the draw, having not done so in the previous 3 attempts, played in similar conditions.

The Haig increased the velocity of the wind as Young Gary looked up the hole.

"What do you think?" He asked his Dad.

"I think we need to hit a draw," said AGS.

"Ok," he said, and he did.

The draw took hold, assisted by the wind. It landed in the middle of the fairway, bounced left, and ran. When it came to rest, it had just fallen into the only bunker on the left side of the fairway.

There was only one option, pitch out to the fairway. Three shots later, a bogey was secured. The tension was starting to build.

11th hole, Gene was in charge. Old Tom and Bob were standing beside him.

"What are you thinking Gene?" asked Bob, "looks like Young Gary's going on the defensive."

"I agree," said Gene. "I don't have much to play with, apart from the pin being tucked in back right. The hole's playing straight down wind, as long as he avoids the bunkers, par should be straight forward."
Back on the tee, player and caddy were in discussion.

"What have we got?" asked YGS.

"Pin is back right, total yardage 415," said AGS

"What do you see?" asked YGS

"2 options. 4 iron/ 9 iron or driver/ chip and run," said AGS

"What do you like?" asked YGS

"I like option 2, faded driver followed by a chip and run," said AGS, "this is our best hope of a birdie coming in."

Without hesitation, Young Gary pulled out the driver and despatched a beauty to within 10 yards of the green.

"You call that defensive?" laughed Gene. "I wouldn't like to see him in aggressive mode."

Bob just smiled. Two shots later, a birdie was secured. Five shot lead still intact.

12th Hole, Gene was still in charge, exercising his right as a Grand Slam winner. The wind was into from the left.

"This is more like it," he said rubbing his hands.

"The bunkers are well out of range," said AGS, "and so is the green in two."

THE FUNDAMENTAL TRUTH

"What do you see?" asked YGS.

"We've got a 5 shot lead and a 5 will do nicely here. I see low, low and low," said AGS.

5 shots later, par was secured.

"He's too good this kid," moaned Gene, "reminds me of me." They all laughed.

13th hole, Arnold had been drafted in late as nearly all the Mischief Makers had departed to the Carnoustie Ladies Golf Club where, "The Haig" was in charge of, 'entertainment'."

"Thanks for stepping in Arnold" said Bob, "Old Tom, Ben and
I are the only ones left, Walter will have a lot of explaining to do when this is finished."

"No problem Bob," said Arnold, "you know how I like the 13th hole. Don't be too hard on Walter". His on course mischief was done.

"It's the guys who have abandoned their posts from here on in that should be in trouble. They may come back in time to carry out their duties."

"Don't bet on it," said Old Tom, "we had a similar situation here back in '68. It was 'the sixties man', flower power, free love and all that stuff."

The Members were not prepared for that. Young Tom was in charge of clubhouse mischief, his last year before Walter took over. His on course duties finished on the 10th that year, there was only me and Willie Park left to complete the round"..........

The pin on the par three was back right. The wind was into the players, from the right, gusting up to 25mph.

"What have we got?" asked YGS.

"Adjusted for the wind, 195 to the pin, 185 to carry the right hand bunker," said AGS

"How far to carry the bunkers at the front of the green?" asked YGS.

"160 adjusted," said AGS.

Young Gary pulled out a 5-iron. Arnold hesitated, Bob smiled, Arnold knew that nothing he would do with the wind would affect Gary's shot choice, apart from changing the wind direction by more than 25 degrees, a practice strictly frowned on by the committee.

It was ok for such an adjustment to be made as the tide turned at sea, or overnight, but not on a shot to shot basis. Young Gary made his move.

"That swing reminds me of a certain Mr Trevino," said Arnold. "See how he caressed the ball."

The ball took off as if in slow motion, it barely rose above 20ft, landed 5 yards on and released to within 25ft of the pin, 2 putts secured the par. Still 15 under.

The roars up ahead confirmed that birdies were starting to appear all over the last 5 holes. Old Tom and Bob went up ahead to investigate.

Sure enough, although Committee Members were back in

place, the mischief making was being neglected. There were huddles all over the last 5 holes and nobody was watching the golf.

Walter's exploits were the distraction. Bob and Tom moved quickly to address the situation.

"You should know better gentlemen," said Bob, "you're behaving like a group of adolescent teenagers."

"Sorry Bob," said Jimmy D. "Walter was pretty persuasive when he left the 10th green. We didn't realise you would be left short-handed, we should have checked in with you and Tom first. Henry here should have been on 13, he miss-calculated when he could leave the party. We're all in place now."

14th hole, Bob took over. This par 5, although short by modern standards, was today, a severe test. Young Gary's lead was down to 3 shots.

"What do you see?" asked YGS.

"The wind's changing," said AGS. "Your fade won't get you close enough to take on the specs and the third shot over them is no bargain in this wind. The pin today is tucked in behind the bunker on the right. If your lay-up is 25 or 30 yards short of the Specs, you'll have 140 left to the pin.

He looked over at his son. "As you know, you can't see the pin and you can't feel the strength of the wind when you're that close. When you're that close you have to elevate the shot, which will stall in the wind and require more club. Then you're open to all kinds of mischief."

Young Gary laughed, "So, what do you see?"

"I see a low raking hook starting just left of the trees." Said AGS

"Ok," said YGS.

The Mischief Makers looked on.

"Nice once Bob," said Byron.

"Sometimes you just have to hit the draw," smiled Bob.

They all laughed.

Young Gary teed up on the extreme left of the tee, his feet were outside the teeing ground. He made his move, GP had shown him. He knew what to do.

The ball flew pretty straight for the first 150 yards, them the wind and spin started to take effect. The ball landed about 230 and released another 40, coming to rest 15ft adjacent to the last left hand fairway bunker.

"Shot son," said AGS, The Mischief Makers were all smiling. When they reached the ball, the wind was into the players, off the right, steady at about 18mph.

"What have we got?" asked YGS

"We've got 235 adjusted, to clear the specs," Said AGS

"What do you see?" asked YGS

"I see a four wood hit low, just clearing the specs by about 15ft, slight fade, landing on the down slope, releasing onto the middle of the green," Said AGS

"I like it," said Young Gary. He made his move, two putts later, a birdie was secured.

15th Hole, Henry was waiting. The wind was the same as 14. The bunkers this time were on the right.

"What do you see?" asked YGS.

"The pin here is short left, but ultimately the middle of the green is our target. I see the same drive as you hit at the last, starting on the last bunker on the right." Said AGS

"Ok," replied YGS. Henry was listening in and decided to keep his mischief on hold, for the next shot. Young Gary executed the draw to perfection. They both looked at the scoreboard as they left the tee, still 3 in front.

Henry saw to it that the drive ended up in a divot. The boos rang out from the assembled Mischief Makers. Henry just shrugged. Auld Gary could see the lie as they approached.

"Looks like your options will be limited on your next shot." he said. Young Gary sighed as he approached the ball.

"You're not wrong Dad," he said as he pulled a 2-iron from the bag and addressed the ball. He made his move and the ball was dispatched towards the target. It eventually pulled up 20 yards short of the green, but smack in the middle of the fairway.

Henry seemed a little frustrated, as he hadn't had time to create any more mischief, before the shot had been played.

"Slowcoach!" laughed Jimmy. Henry, feeling embarrassed, simply shrugged again and strode off in the direction of the green.

Father and son strode briskly towards the ball and were already agreeing on shot selection, an 8 iron chip using the shoulder of the bunker to throw the ball onto the slope which would feed towards the pin. Execution was swift and accurate, par was secured.

16th hole. Seve's turn. The wind was picking up, significantly.
"Reminds me of Lytham in '79," he said with a grin.

"He'll need his driver," said Arnold, "and there's no carpark bail out here." Seve laughed along with the rest.

"I was playing free Arnold," he retorted.

Again there was no choice for Young Gary as he stood on the tee. The driver was selected, the move was made, the ball flight a little higher and cutting into the wind.
It landed softly at the front of the green. Two putts later, par was secured. A roar erupted from the 17th green. The lead was down to 2.

17th hole, Dwight was given the honour.

The "island" between the loops in the Barry Burn was the normal landing spot for tee shots leaving something like 200 yards to the green.

Today the wind was strong behind and off the left. The previous players had carried the loop with their driver as they attempted to catch the leader.

"What do you see?" asked Young Gary.
"Downwind, 4-iron, 4-iron," said AGS.

THE FUNDAMENTAL TRUTH

"Ok," replied Young Gary. 10 minutes later a par was secured.

Dwight shrugged, "I didn't have any trees," he said. They all laughed.

18th Hole, Ben was waiting.

Standing with him, were two people he did not expect, Gary's grannie Glenda and his daughter Olivia.

Ben told Glenda that he was in charge of mischief on this hole and wondered if she had any ideas.

"I don't know much about golf Ben," she said "but if he's anything like his Dad he'll create his own mischief without any outside help."

Ben laughed, knowing the truth of that statement. He wouldn't interfere, the 18th at Carnoustie, into the wind is about as fearsome as a golf hole can get. The crowd was earily silent as the players walked onto the tee.

"What have we got?" asked YGS.

"A bloody long way," said AGS.

"What do you see?" asked YGS laughing.

"We play for a five and we win by one," said AGS.

A 2-iron, an 8-iron, an 8-iron and two putts later, Young Gary Shepherd was the winner of the gold medal, and the champion golfer of the year.

The cheers and the applause seemed to go on forever, father and son hugging, tears flowing.

They spotted Ben at the side of the green, Glenda and Olivia were gone. Glenda thought it would be too much for Young Gary to witness with the whole world watching. They would visit later. Much later.

In the Caley Club after the Party, both Committees gathered for the feedback on this year's mischief making performance.

It was agreed that Walter be made permanent clubhouse mischief maker following his outstanding performance this week. Bob shook his head and sighed.

18

AUGUSTA GEORGIA DECEMBER 2024

President Elect, Tiger Woods had invited outgoing President, Donald Trump to a friendly four-ball at Augusta National to discuss the handover of the keys to the Oval Office.

Joining them were former First Minister for Scotland, Alec Cargill, and the evergreen Gary Player. 4 golf balls were thrown up in the air to decide on the pairings.

It would be the two Presidents against the two Amigos.

"Kinda like the Pryderent Cup," said Donald laughing, "what are the stakes?"

"The usual," said Alec, "a bottle of Speyside malt."

Tiger, in the intervening years since President Trump's election and subsequent discoveries, had given up thoughts of returning to the PGA Tour and had dedicated himself to his Foundation.

The incredible advances in medical science as a result of the exponential growth in Artificial Intelligence (A.I.) had tempted him, as he was now back at the fitness levels of 2003.

He however, like everyone else on the planet, realised that the pursuit of personal goals, were no longer relevant. The global goal, the survival of the human race, now occupied every one's mind.

When, in California early in 2016, it was discovered how to alter the Earth's climate, the information was so sensitive, no one outside a small group of scientists could be trusted.

Once the A.I. was sufficiently advanced (which occurred in February 2017), the then President could be told of the discovery.

The standard of Tiger's golf was now so high it took 10 minutes to negotiate the stroke allowance. They finally settled on 6 each for Gary and Alec and an extra 2 for Donald.

Knowing the mind games normally associated with four-ball matches, Donald decided not to inform his partner of the issues he would face when he entered the White House - he needed unimpeded focus for the next 4 hours.

They started in glorious sunshine, a balmy 23 deg.

"What a beautiful day," announced Gary. "Reminds me of home in South Africa."

"It should do," said Donald. "Balance is returning to the climate, I just need to get some balance in my golf swing."

The match commenced and it was a pretty close affair as they approached the 11th. The Mischief Making committee were out in force, looking to banish the post-Thanksgiving blues.

"It's your call Sam," said Bob, "Tiger and Donald are

2-up, what do you think?"

"Donald's been itching to tell Tiger about what he can expect when he enters the Oval Office, but he thinks it may upset him, and he wants to win this match real bad," said Sam.

GP overheard this and decided to step in.

"Hey Donald," he said, "I hear the job of President is a lot easier now with all that A.I. at your disposal."

"Fake news," said Donald staring at GP, "what did you hear specifically, and from whom?"

GP laughed, "I was on Twitter, a little bird told me. He said Donald just plays golf all day, A.I. now run the White House." Silence.

"Is that true?" asked Tiger.

"I'm afraid so," said Donald. "They've been in charge since '22."

Tiger was visibly upset. "So what does that mean for me?" he asked.

"It's not so bad," said Donald, "you'll be able to resume your pursuit of Jack's tally of majors. Your priority, of course, will be your Foundation. Our bosses, I mean our friends in A.I. have agreed that education is the key to success for the human race. Your sustainable programme will be run out across the planet. That should keep you busy."

Alec and Gary were smiling. They knew the Tiger spell had been broken. The water beckoned on 11, 12 and 13. Gary and Alec were 1 up.

"Ok Bob," said Byron, "over to you."

"I think I'll leave them," said Bob, "losing 3 in a row will free Tiger up, and I feel a Donald tweet coming up."

"So Alec" said Donald. "I hear the Arbroath Smokie is going to be outlawed due to the pollution it's creating."

The Arbroath Smokie was barrel smoked haddock, exported all over the world and a particular favourite of Alec Cargill.

"Never happen," said Alec, "haddock stocks are at record levels now that automated farming techniques are fully operational. Our A.I. friends are encouraging the increase in production. They say it's a food source that keeps the population healthy and compliant."

"I know," said Donald, "but the air quality in the Arbroath area is some of the worst on the planet. Surely that must upset you."

"It does Donald, but the carbon capture scheme will be fully operational within two months, the problem will go away."

"Good try Donald," said Gary recognising the attempt at mischief, "but I'm from South Africa, the problems with The Smokie don't affect me."

"I heard Sun City was being returned to the wild. Our A.I. friends don't approve of casinos. I've long ago had to give up my family's business interests in gambling. Las Vegas's casinos are all gone."

"I agree," laughed Gary. The 14th was halved in 4.

Gene hitched up his plus fours and got to work on 15. All four players were fully focused, as all three had shots on Tiger, who'd hit a long one, finishing adjacent to the copse of trees on the left.

The other three were about 50 yards back, some 230 yards from the green. This was "the shot heard around the world territory" and Gene cut the wind completely, it was cathedral quiet. Donald was away at 235 yards out. Tiger advised him to lay-up, which he did. Alec did the same.

Gary, however, had no intention of laying up, the draw he hit was as natural as walking to him, Gene blew a little from behind, and the ball just fell off the back, leaving a chip up the hill to a downhill green. Tiger took a little off a 7-iron and landed front middle before releasing to 12ft.

The Mischief Makers were deliberately keeping out of sight, there were other goals to be achieved here today and they didn't want the A.I. community to be aware of their presence.

Since the take-over world-wide 2 years previously, Mischief Makers had gone underground, only appearing to humans when they were sure they could not be monitored.

With the pressure off, both Alec and Donald smoothed in a couple of gap wedges to 8ft. Gary knew he could be aggressive with his chip as birdies were guaranteed for each team.

He selected an 8-iron as he wanted it running at pace, minimising the effect of the break. He judged it beautifully, he knew if it missed the pin it would end up in the water, but it didn't miss. Gene just smiled. 1 up with 3 to play.

Jimmy D sat in his usual spot humming his tune. Today

he was resplendent in a Stars and Stripes outfit in honour of the two Presidents, three if he included Dwight. Just as well he couldn't be seen as the glare from his persona would have lit up a football field.

The pin was in the Masters Sunday location back left. An easy position for the draw, provided the correct club was selected. Jimmy started making mischief, the players looked confused on the tee.

Alec hit first, taking enough club to finish in the middle of the green, some 30ft short of the pin. Gary hit the same shot with one more club and finished 12ft short, leaving an uphill putt. Tiger took a more aggressive line and finished 10ft above the pin.

Donald was up last. He was playing with real freedom today, knowing that his Presidency was coming to an end. He made his move, the draw took, the first bounce was high right which took the pace off.

The second and third bounces brought the ball almost to a standstill, before starting to trickle, slowly gaining pace as it hit the slope, moving inexorably towards the hole, and in. Roars on the tee.

"Nice work Jimmy," said Bob.

"Thanks Bob," said Jimmy. "Haven't seen Tiger for a while, thought I'd give him a reminder of the chip in I gave him in '05."

"Yeah, that was a beaut," laughed Bob. All square.

Dwight was up ahead weighing up his options. He wanted to make mischief here, that would not just affect this little encounter, but would send the four on a journey that would have (he hoped) a serious impact on the future of humanity.

As the players stepped on to the tee, he began to make the trees sway in the wind, not too much, as he knew A.I. would be watching, they had eyes everywhere.

"Isn't that beautiful?" said Gary. "The trees are dancing for us". He knew that there was mischief afoot.

Alec and Gary, along with Ian and AGS had been working with the Mischief Makers committees, covertly over the last 2 years.

It was hoped that today's game would bring Tiger and Donald on board. They had to be convinced that A.I. although seemingly benevolent towards the human race, were controlling our freedoms.

It was they after all, who reversed global warming, with the polar region ice making technology, basically using the sun's energy to convert liquid water into ice.

That, combined with the mass migration of humans (now underway) away from the tropical zones to the temperate zones, had given the planet a chance of sustainability for centuries to come.

"It's like they're whispering," said Alec.

"Fake news," laughed Donald. "You guys keep trying, but there's no doubt who's got the momentum now. Look at my partner, he's got his game face on, this match is toast."

Tiger swung away and sent a rocket straight down the middle of the fairway. Donald, still chattering, followed suit although some 80 yards back. Gary stepped up as the wind suddenly picked up from behind. He made his move, the ball soared, carried on the wind, pitched beside Tiger's and eased forward another 10 yards.

"Wow" said Donald. "What was that?!"

"More fake news," laughed Gary.

Alec followed suit, with a similar result. The wind fell away and the trees resumed their whispering. Tiger was a little shaken, he looked over to Donald.

"Looks like these guys have got some outside help," he said. "I've never seen a wind pick up so quickly."

"Could be our friends in A.I. having a little fun with us," said Donald. "You wouldn't believe some of the stuff I've seen over the last few years.

They're still experimenting with the climate, the air masses are becoming more stable, extreme weather events are reducing month on month."

"I guess I'll find out soon enough," said Tiger. "Anything else I should know?"

"They only tell me a little so I can tweet the population, but be assured, they are exploring all avenues in their relentless pursuit of knowledge. My duties post White House are all laid out for me. I'm to be in charge of the creation of golf communities throughout the planet, develop the art of tweeting to send subliminal messages which will help control the more radical elements of humanity."

"Ok fellas" said Gary, "we've got a game to finish, let's

THE FUNDAMENTAL TRUTH

talk after the game."

And they did.

19

AUGUSTA   GEORGIA   2034

(Meeting of The Masters Mischief Making Committee)

"Good morning gentlemen," said chairman Bob. "100 years ago I welcomed my friends from around the world to celebrate the first playing of the Masters Tournament.

We've witnessed many great events here over the years, and this committee has played a major role in helping the Masters achieve it's now almost mythical status." Tapping of glasses and stamping of feet.

"The changes we've witnessed over recent years weigh heavily on all of us here present, indeed, although our tournament is no longer part of the PGA tour, which itself no longer exists, it is still a very prestigious event and a cornerstone of the Grand Slam which, thankfully, has been allowed to continue."

"Golf, it seems gentlemen, is a pursuit that the A.I. community sees as a fundamental building block for the future of mankind."

Smiles around the room.

"We here must ensure that the mischief we create is seen to comply with A.I.'s aims and goals until humanity gets organised and can make their own assessment of life under A.I.'s supervision."

"First order of business gentlemen, is the review of our qualification guidelines, given the new set of circumstances, in which we now operate. Since the demise of all professional sports and indeed, all professional activity, humanity is slowly adjusting to life without paid employment. Guideline 3 is now obsolete which leaves only 1 and 2 as viable routes to membership, unless of course we decide to introduce further guidelines.

Recreation, Education or 'RE' as A.I. prefer to call it is the intended occupation for 98 percent of humanity from birth to death. We're not sure at this time what is intended for the remaining 2 percent.

Please take time to consider the possibility that membership of this committee may have to move away from pure golfing achievements, Dwight here being a perfect example."

Dwight indicated that he would like to say a few words, Bob nodded and sat down.

"As we know, the honorary starters for the Masters, Gary and Jack, will be joined for the first time by former President, Tiger Woods, who retired from office in January 2033 after 8 years in charge.

Tiger through his Foundation has been instrumental in keeping the human race informed and educated with regard to their new situation.

His cover as a starter will keep him under the radar, so he and Gary can develop future plans without A.I. being aware.

Obviously communication has to be old school, hand written where appropriate, visual signals and body language otherwise."

"Our three starters are all eligible for our committee through guidelines 1 and 2 with Jack and Tiger also eligible under 3. We look forward to welcoming them when the time comes."

"At this time I see no need to reinstate former guideline 4."

"Ok Dwight" said Bob, "thanks for that, given the historic occasion, I now call on our first 3-time winner, Jimmy D to say a few words."

"Thank you Bob" said Jimmy. "Well gentlemen, 100 years of Masters Golf… I remember the first Masters I attended. Magnolia Lane was .. magnolificent. The azaleas were, well azealicious , and the greens were.. my worst nightmare!"

Laughter.

"They were so fast, I wore crampons instead of spikes! Crampons were allowed as long as they were green. I saw a weed once and reported it and the whole place went into lockdown. It was so hot that year the players deliberately hit balls into the lakes so they could dive in and recover their balls!"

I went into a rest room.."

"Thanks Jimmy" interrupted Bob, "the second order of business is the allocation of holes."

****

Meanwhile, in the Butler Cabin, Tiger, Jack and Gary were having breakfast.

THE FUNDAMENTAL TRUTH

Over the last decade, the Tiger Woods Foundation had grown exponentially and had now replaced the formal education system world-wide.

"Jobs" as they used to be known, no longer existed, all tasks formerly undertaken by humans, were now carried out by robots and computers.

Humans did interact with machines and computers, mainly to further enhance their knowledge of each other. President Trump, in his 8 years in office had, with A.I.'s assistance, changed the world beyond all recognition.

With his ingenious use of Twitter, he was able to defeat terrorism within the first two years, the knock on effect of which was the ending of all organised religion. Imagine that.

President Trump knew that saving the planet was the only religion worth fighting for and the scientific discoveries which made the reversal of global warming achievable, meant that he could set about making it happen.

Two things were fundamental to the process in order for it to succeed. Firstly, the human population had to be reduced and secondly, the population had to move.

With A.I.'s guidance the first of these would be relatively simple to achieve. Every human was given access to Twitter whenever and wherever they needed it, which was basically all the time, birth-rates fell dramatically.

Human brain development also reduced the amount of sexual activity. A.I.'s stated objective was to improve brain function in humans to an optimum 50 percent of capacity.

This would be 5 times greater than pre-A.I. levels. This improvement, A.I. believed, would help humanity adjust to their new status, with the minimum of stress.

Moving the population out of the tropic and Polar Regions of the planet would be a little more challenging and would happen over a much longer time scale.

New communities in the temperate zones would be created, therefore construction on an unprecedented scale would be required.

"So Tiger," asked Jack, "how is your Foundation progressing now that you're retired?"

"Pretty good Jack," said Tiger. "As you know, President Trump managed to create over 100,000 golf courses world-wide over the last 10 years, with you and Gary's help of course. Each golf course has had 1000 trees planted, which, if my maths are correct is 10 million trees. The irrigation of the northern Sahara Desert is progressing well, so we should be able to start construction of another 100,000 courses in the region early next year."

"The migration north and south out of tropical Africa is well under way with over 2 million spread along the North African coast. Over 1 million have moved to South Africa where 10,000 golf courses are being constructed. As we know, each golf course and the surrounding environment is designed to support a community of 5,000 humans, 1000 of whom are active golfers. The remainder are free to choose their own hobbies from the approved list."

He took a sip of his tea and continued.

"With the birth and death rates trending towards 1 per day of each, for each community, sustainability is now the most important and frequently used communitive term, hobbies such as farming and hunting are encouraged on a sustainable level."

He glanced around the room taking in the calm atmosphere.

"Competition in the communities is restricted to sport and games. All previous human sports and games are allowed apart from weaponised activity and fighting. New sports and games have been developed which our A.I. friends hope will increase human brain activity. 50 percent of brain capacity is expected to be the norm in 25 years. Inter-community competition will be encouraged, as will normal human movement, once the communities are established."

"Good way of learning about different communities I guess," said Gary.

"My Global Foundation focuses on education, mostly on the relationship between humans and A.I. Although the communities are designed to be self-sufficient it's important to maintain harmony between the two communities."

He went on; "We don't want humanity to become obsolete, and neither do our friends. At least that's what they told me. Tiger Universities will continue to focus on the needs of both, so that we can co-habit this planet in harmony until our sun starts to expand. The target human population is 7.2 billion which we think is par for the course, I mean planet."

Gary and Jack laughed.

"It's been confirmed through research that 20 percent

of the population will want to be active golfers, some 1,440,000,000 swingers. This means we need to construct another 1,300,000 golf courses."

"The process is now fully mechanised, but we still need the human touch as demonstrated by yourselves in all corners of the temperate zones. With your help and that of many other renowned architects, former President Trump estimates that 2052 should see the task complete."

"I'm concentrating on the Sahara at the moment" said Gary, "the creation of 100 fresh water lakes each 100 miles long by 20 miles wide has changed the desert beyond all recognition. It's now a very green and pleasant land which is prime for golf course construction. Unlimited water from the Mediterranean Sea with each lake having a desalination plant on the coast – it's an Architects dream.

"I'm informed that I can shape the land and use as much water as I need to create features. Each lake will supply 1000 golf courses and surrounding environment through a series of canals and solar powered pumping stations."

"I'm heading east," said Jack, "because of the huge population, China has the most pressing need for diversification. They have grown the game exponentially over the last decade and at last count they had over 50,000 golf courses all located within 400 miles of the east coast."

He drained his teacup before continuing.

"The demand for space here is so intense, given the density of population there. The only option is to build the other 200,000 courses out west into Xinjiang, Tibet and Qinghai provinces, which is an area even bigger than your Sahara Gary and a lot higher up."

"Yeah, yeah," said Gary with a hint of sarcasm. "Always needs to feel he's got the biggest and the best projects. He's still chasing Majors, Tiger."

Jack, unfazed, continued. "The major problem, similar to the one in the Sahara, is the lack of water. Our friends in A.I. due to their work on the climate came up with an ingenious solution. The proximity of the Himalaya and the permanent snow cover was a ready-made storage tank. Although of finite size, it's still pretty big."

"Everything above 6000m was white permanently, they've now managed to create almost permanent snowing conditions on the north facing slopes down to the Tibetan Plateau. New rivers have been excavated, all heading north. I also have a green and pleasant land in which to work."

"I know that over 200 million Chinese have already headed west seeking a less congested existence," said Tiger. "You'd better get a move on Jack."

They all laughed.

****

Meanwhile back at the committee meeting.

"The field this year gentlemen includes many more former champions due to the improvement in healthcare. All the surviving champions dating back to the sixties are back in the field except for Jack, Gary and Tiger who as we know, are otherwise engaged."

"27 former winners are here including two 97 year olds, Tommy Arron and Charles Coody who are playing super seniors golf to a very good standard. The remaining 63 invitees are former professional and amateur champions, only 10 of whom haven't played before. Given this knowledge are there any members who wish to change their normal hole allocation this year?"

They all looked at each other anticipating someone to make a move. No one blinked.

"Ok gentlemen," said Bob, "the tradition is maintained, the hole allocation is as normal."

"If I may Mr. Chairman," inquired Gene, "it's been 17 long years since our last inductee joined this esteemed body of mischief makers. Is there any prospect of any new members joining us in the foreseeable future?"

"It has been a long time hasn't it?" replied Bob. "Unfortunately no new prospective members have appeared on the scene, Tiger remains the last Grand Slam winner and Phil remains the last three time champion."

"Barring accidents or homicide, Gary will be our next inductee in April 2051. That's when his maximum 115 year life expectancy will mature.

I'm afraid gentlemen, as I said earlier; we may have to create new categories if we wish to increase membership before then.

Rory's back to try again, but I don't hold out much hope since the leprechauns invaded here back in '21. Usually they just mind their own business but when Irish men are involved they can't help themselves. Remember Shane Lowry at the '16 U.S. Open?"

Murmurs of acknowledgement.

"Ok gentlemen, anything else?" asked Bob.

Stunned silence.

"I agree, we need a drink," smiled Bob. "Where's the whisky?"

"Coming right up," said Jimmy D. "I thought the Knockando would be appropriate given the dilemma we now find ourselves in."

A few titters burst out around the table.

The post meeting informalities would go on long into the night.

20

ARBROATH   JULY   2034

Ian Beattie's daughters, Karen, Louise and Christine had become involved with their Dad's consultative roll back in 2022 when the Grand Plan for the Planet, or the GPP as former marketing expert Karen preferred to call it, was the only game in town.

Karen knew the value of branding and worked hard behind the scenes supporting her Dad and his Amigos in their projects with the then President Trump.

On her numerous visits to Washington, Karen and her sisters - with Mum Elaine riding shotgun - worked the hill like seasoned veterans.

Elaine had visited DC every 2 years since 1972 taking school trips from Arbroath Academy. As a history teacher, she enthused her pupils on American history and generally loved, "Americana".

She knew every building intimately and understood what made Washington tick.

Karen, born in 1984, had just turned 50 and was as enthusiastic today as she was when she graduated from Glasgow University in '05.

Like her Dad she could be very persuasive when arguing for something she believed in. The GPP was an evolving entity and Karen, like her Dad, wanted to keep the evolution from becoming a revolution.

"So Mum" said Karen, "Dad's off to the golf to watch Young Gary practice for the Open, what do you want to do today?"

"When the cat's away...." said Elaine. "Let's take a look at the GPP files and see if we can use our intuition to really look at what our friends have been up to these past 12 years."

"Dad will know we've been looking, and so will our friends. Our computer will report back on every file opened, every word read."

"That's the intention, I'm just and old history teacher looking at historical documents. Dad indicated in his own coded way that we should do it, as he more than anyone, recognises our unique talents for uncovering the hidden agenda behind any action plan, particularly, a GRAND action plan."

"Ooooh," said Karen. "Let's get started."

And they did....

****

Meanwhile, at Carnoustie.

"So son, you want to caddy for your Dad at the Open?" asked YGS.

"Yes please Dad," said George. Although only 14 years old George Shepherd had been golfing with his Dad for nearly ten years.

Already a scratch golfer, George had all the moves required to progress to the highest level of golfing competition, although it was still unclear what that would be.

Apart from the 4 major tournaments, A.I. considered international competition the best way to develop the game at the speed they desired.

Every nation state was expected to send a 20 person team every month to the nation of choice to compete for a week. This amounted to just under 5000 players.

A.I. were happy to allow "Nations" over and above the existing ones, to develop largely without interference, as it encouraged a sense of belonging in humanity.

As organised religions were now obsolete, many groups of like-minded humans felt the need to belong to something other than the local community. It was expected that up to 1000 Nations would exist when the communities were fully established.

These Nations wouldn't be geographic, there would be no borders in the Temperate zone. All humans would be free to choose the Nation to which they felt most closely aligned and would be free to move to other Nations as they developed both physically and emotionally.

The ability to move of course would require space being available in other Nations. The evolution of these new entities would develop naturally over the years.

It was hoped by A.I. that the human brain would develop to a point that the idea of Nationhood itself would be obsolete, but they recognised in the GPP that many generations would come and go before that goal was achievable.

"Ok son," said YGS, "I'm sure your Grandad will be happy to retire from his caddying duties at the Open. He is getting on a bit and although he's very fit for a 91 year old, he doesn't see the shots as well as he used to."

"He is," said George. "We spoke about it last week and he told me not to tell you, he would speak to you himself later today."

A quizzical look descended over Young Gary's face.

"Is there anything else you and your Grandad discussed?"

"Well" said George, "we talked about the book and Hogan's legacy. We also read it together, Grandad quizzed me on Hogan's fundamentals. I think he was testing me."

"You're not wrong George, I got the same treatment when I was your age. Grandad and his two pals read the book for the first time together when they were only a little older than you. He's always looked on it as a sort of guide for life. Ben Hogan lost his father when he was only a young boy. Grandad believes that the writing of the book allowed Hogan to express himself in a way he couldn't before."

He looked over at his son. "The trauma of the loss of his father shaped Ben in a particular way. Grandad believes that he drew into himself and formed characteristics which were fundamental to his ultimate success."

George looked on with interest.

"When Grandad met Ben in 1953 he was a very open and engaging man. The horrific car accident Ben survived in '49 had given him the space to re-evaluate his life, and the characteristics he had developed as a young man gave him the drive to recover and go on to be great champion golfer."

George looked at his Dad for a moment before saying, "I won't have these characteristics will I Dad, I mean nothing bad has ever happened to me."

Dad smiled at his son who was looking a little sad, "Not yet son, but life has a way of creating obstacles and adversity, the important thing is to nurture the tools required to help you deal with those situations. You had a sister, son and although you never knew her, I know that you feel her presence. All your young life you have used that feeling to help you become the fine young man that you are today."

"Remember your Grandad lost his Dad when he was only two and he developed the same characteristics as Hogan, strength of will, determination and unlimited work ethic. No challenge was too great. Anything was achievable with hard work. Your Grandad instilled that in me through encouragement and demonstration. Hogan's book of course has been a friend to us both all our lives. I don't think you'll have a problem with application of these characteristics, wherever your journey takes you."

George looked thoughtful.

"Talking of application, pick up the bag son, let's play golf."

****

THE FUNDAMENTAL TRUTH

The Open was to be held this year on the new Trump's Triumph links at Barry Buddon.

The whole Buddon sand belt was now covered in golf courses, integrated with hotels, housing and other sporting arenas.

When A.I. saw the growth in Donald Trump's business empire and specifically the golf resort developments, they immediately recognised that this was the opportunity they sought to put their Grand Plan for the Planet into action.

A.I. ensured that Donald Trump would become the 45th President of the USA. On the day Donald entered the White House, they knew they were unstoppable.

Humanity was in for a big surprise.

Young Gary and George arrived at the TT, as the new golf course was affectionately known. Designed by Gary Player the 7200 yard layout was hailed around the world as a classic and would ultimately be copied extensively throughout the Temperate zone as climatic conditions stabilised.

The design philosophy was to maximise the benefits of the terrain. In TT's case it was easy to re-shape the sand dunes to suit the 4 par 5, 10 par 4 and 4 par 3 layouts.

Gary's idea was to have each of the par 5's and par 3's orientated broadly north, south, east and west. The course started with the shortest par 5 at 552 yards heading north away from the clubhouse. The second hole was a par 3 heading back towards the clubhouse.

The course layout looked like a wheel with 6 holes in each quadrant and the clubhouse being the hub.

The benefit of this layout was obvious. No part of the course was further than 600 yards from the clubhouse and the potential for variance in the playability of each hole was limitless. Depending on the prevailing wind conditions, each hole could employ most of the clubs in the bag.

Waiting for Young Gary and George was the man himself.
GP had finished his warm up and was standing beside the first tee, waiting as arranged.

"Hello Gary my friend," said GP, as YGS and George approached. "This must be George," he said offering his hand.

George smiled looking GP in the eye as he accepted the warm handshake and said, "Very pleased to meet you at long last Mr Player."

"Like wise George," said GP. "I've heard a lot about you from your Grandad, he tells me your move is as good as it gets. Come on over and show me."

As two former champions, YGS and GP could now have guest players and friends play a few holes in practice on any Open venue.

George took out his Dad's driver, spent a good minute stretching and getting a feel for the club which was the same model as his own.

THE FUNDAMENTAL TRUTH

YGS looked on with great pride as his son teed up and looked up the first hole from behind the ball. It was eerily silent as he walked towards the ball.

Ben was looking on, smiling at GP and YGS. George made his move.

At 14 years of age George's body was growing rapidly, his move reflected the flexibility of his frame, the ball was despatched with great authority down the left side of the opening par 5.

"Beautiful drive George" said GP, "you've been coached very well."

"I read the book with my Grandad," said George.

"As every young man should," smiled GP. "How's the Hogan Heritage Centre doing Young Gary?" knowing that Ben was listening in. "I haven't been back at Carnoustie since '18. Too busy building new golf courses."

"It's going great," said YGS. "New students arrive at 100 per month. It takes 4 weeks then we send them out to you guys in the field where they practice like Ben to perfect the move. When they're ready they take up residency at one of the new courses. Ben sits in with the students at the back of the lecture room he makes mischief with the students if he feels they aren't focused enough."

George looked puzzled. "Ben who?" he asked.

"We just know him as Ben" said YGS aware that he'd said too much. "He's a training consultant, kind of like the guy from the Star Wars Movies Ben Kenobi."

George knew his Dad well enough to know when he

was being evasive, but he also knew with the exchange of glances that he shouldn't pursue the matter.

"I remember these movies" he said, "they were great."

"Ok," said GP, "let's play golf, what do you say George?"

"I'm ready Mr Player."

"I know you are son, I know you are."

And they did.

****

Meanwhile, back in Arbroath, the Beattie household was alive with chatter about the GPP.

"This is an amazing piece of work," said Elaine, "historically speaking…" knowing that A.I. were listening in.

"It was conceived back in 2020 when Donald was President and is, like any document of significance, devoid of lawyer speak. The language used gets straight to the point. The reader is left in no doubt what the aims and goals of the plan are," said Elaine.

Karen concurred, understanding the message her mother was passing on. "I need some fresh air, let's go for a walk along the cliffs."

When they got to the cliffs there was a slight breeze from the sea. The haddock fish farms stretched all the way out to the Bell Rock lighthouse and beyond. The offshore Smokie factory at 15 miles out could be seen on the horizon.

"It has to be out there," said Elaine knowing they couldn't be observed out here, or so she thought. "The smoke has to be the key. The skin of the haddock absorbs the smoke which dries it out and thickens it.

As you lean over the Smokie picking the flesh off the bones, you are exposed to the smell of smoked flesh. This has a calming effect on the brain, kind of the same effect as smoking a bee-hive."

"So what you're saying Mum is that the major aim of the GPP is to keep the human race compliant through the use of some additive in the smoking process of haddock."

"It looks like it to me," said Elaine. "The terms and language used in the plan seem to relegate humans from their perception as the prime inhabitants of the planet to just another air breathing mammal."

"Why do you think they want that?" asked Karen.

"It seems to me that A.I. consider themselves as the prime inhabitants, they do all the work now so they see us like pets, to entertain them but not to compete with them."

"So that's the reason for the additive," said Karen, "to keep our more aggressive tendencies in check."

"That, plus the sporting competition. Golf in particular is played well when the mind is calm. It is however one of the most frustrating sports and is seen as a vehicle for de-stressing. All the aggression is removed by the process of hitting that little white ball."

"Of course," said Karen laughing. "Mental torture

brings tranquillity and the other sports like rugby and football bring physical as well as mental pain, for those who need it."

"Exactly" said Elaine. "All human activity is now designed to keep us calm, which, on the surface at least, is no bad thing. If A.I. hadn't intervened, the planet was on a collision course. Plastics were destroying the oceans, population growth was out of control and resources were being decimated."

"So," said Karen, "what's the problem? Everything in the garden seems rosy, the population is being reduced, the planet is being brought back into balance, people are going to live healthy contented lives until they reach 115, what's wrong with that?"

"The problem, as I see it" said Elaine, "is that throughout human history, mankind has fought against being subservient to anyone or anything, but through conditioning, that is exactly what is being proposed."

"Surely" said Karen, "our friends will recognise that, 'trait' if you will and take steps to manage it."

"No doubt about it," said Elaine. "At the moment they need us to be a little aggressive in our approach in order that they can continue to evolve themselves. They, I think are observing our aggression with a view to adopting it into their own DNA if you will."

"Is this what Dad was hoping you would find?"

"I think Dad and his friends already know this, I think he expected us to find the plan within a plan. The question, I believe he is really asking. What will we do with this knowledge?"

THE FUNDAMENTAL TRUTH

"I think I see where he's coming from," said Karen. "The most aggressive side of mankind tends to be male dominated and he wants to get a female perspective on whether mankind should resist this plan or accept our fate. To be glorified pets."

"Not only that," said Elaine. "If A.I. adopt the, 'aggressive gene' into their own DNA, will they use it against us. The plan's stated aim is to help mankind develop their brain function to achieve an efficiency level of at least 50 percent at age 25 by the year 2060. This process alone, they expect, will eliminate the aggressive side of humanity entirely."

"So these higher functioning humans will be entirely compliant and live happy lives, in harmony with the planet for ever and ever," said Karen. "I don't think so."

"The question for us is," said Elaine, "why would A.I. develop our brain capacity to 50 percent plus for us just to live in harmony with the planet. If we were the problem, why not make us extinct."

"So what else do they have in mind?"

"That, Karen is the question for the ages and I think we have to find the answer pretty quick."

"We may find the answer pretty quick" said Karen, "but we may not like the answer. If we assume that is the case, there doesn't appear there is a lot we can do about it."

"It would appear that is the case. However, Dad and his friends may know more, let's go find them."

I. A. SHEPHERD

And they did.

21

AUGUSTA GEORGIA APRIL 2051

(Meeting of The Masters Mischief Makers Committee)

"Welcome gentlemen," said chairman Bob, "this is indeed a day to remember. Our first inductee since 2017. Please be upstanding as we welcome… Mr Gary Player!"

Loud cheers and stamping of feet.

The doors swing open and in walks Gary Player, alongside him, walked Jack Nicklaus.

Stunned silence.

"I know, I know fellas," said Jack, "you weren't expecting me for another 5 years, but, here I am."

"How did that happen Jack?" asked Bob

"Well Bob, as you know, I've had many procedures done to keep this old frame mobile and generally, I was very pleased with the work. The new hands and feet in particular were a benefit to my golf game, giving me an extra 30 yards off the tee. This proved useful when I was testing the 3 new golf courses I was opening every day."

"Anyway, I was on the 16th tee, somewhere in Outer Mongolia. Everywhere looks the same to me now, just one golf course after another and another and…"

He glanced around the room.

"I was going for this big carry over a ravine, a big gust of wind got up, I lost my balance, and down I went. So here I am."

GP was looking particularly sheepish as the committee stared at him.

"Ok I admit it" he said, "I caused the gust of wind, but I only meant for him to fall on the tee, not leap into oblivion."

"Don't worry my friend," said Jack. "I couldn't let you and Arnold here have all the fun. The Big Three are back together again."

Loud cheers and stamping of feet.

"Well gentlemen, that's a bonus," said Bob, "two of our three remaining grand slam winners arrive at the same time. I believe that brings our committee numbers up to 10. Welcome news indeed. Before we celebrate too much gentlemen, Dwight here would like to say a few words."

"Thank you Bob," said Dwight, looking a little sterner than normal. Everyone could sense that he wasn't going to be talking exclusively about the rules of membership.

"Mischief Makers world-wide have, as you know, been observing our friends in A.I. over the last 3 decades, in order to establish what their real intentions are, for the human race."

"The Grand Plan for the Planet is being followed 'religiously' if you'll excuse my use of the term. Human brain development has followed the predicted course, the planet is in balance. The golf course construction phase is almost complete, thanks in no small part to these two

THE FUNDAMENTAL TRUTH

gentlemen here."

Tapping of glasses.

"The population is reducing on schedule and the movement of humanity to the temperate zone is complete."

"It has come to our attention, through our communication with the three amigos, that the experimentation on the criminal element of society, has reached a successful conclusion. The super aggressive gene has been isolated and adapted for use in an A.I. environment."

Worried looks and silence covered the ensemble. Every one present knew what this meant. If A.I. so chose, the more unsavoury character traits of humanity could be spread through-out their community.

"All is not yet lost gentlemen," said Dwight. "We've been waiting for this news for so long that we've forgotten that we Mischief Makers contemplated this scenario some 20 years ago. We just didn't make plans on how to deal with it."

He looked over at the two new arrivals. "We've been waiting for Gary and Jack to arrive in order that a fully thought through strategy could be developed. Let's listen to what they have to say before we descend completely into the gloom."

Gary jumped up. "Wow! I'm loving this new body, although my 114 year old frame was still pretty good - 1000 crunches a day keeps a belly at bay."

Everyone sniggered.

"Malt whisky has the same effect on this body type," laughed Jimmy D. "It's the fuel of the soul, the aphrodisiac of the after-life, it's the mischief-makers muesli, the food of the fornicators, the…"

"Ok Jimmy," interrupted Bob. "Gary please continue."

"Thank you Mr Chairman, " said Gary somewhat sheepishly, still getting used to his new form. "It'll take me a while to get used to the finer points of the Mischief Makers world and I'll take Jimmy's advice on board in due course, probably in the next 10 minutes, especially after having listened to Jack's recount of his great achievements."

Much Laughter and tapping of glasses.

"Jack and I were asked back in '23 by President Trump to help in the Globalisation of Golf. A task if I may say, we were delighted to undertake. Golf has been great to the both of us and anything we could do to help grow the game has always been life goals."

"At first we had no conception of the scale of the task; we already had flourishing golf course design businesses and figured an expansion of our sphere of influence would be achievable and sustainable."

"When President Trump explained the 'reality' of our new situation, Jack and I quickly adjusted our goals. We were sent to parts of the planet where golf had never been heard of, let alone played."

The room stayed quiet.

"In my case the Sahara Desert and in Jack's case The

THE FUNDAMENTAL TRUTH

Tibetan Plateau. These were monumental undertakings, but with A.I. in charge, pretty routine in the execution. We got to know the A.I. community pretty well over the years as you are all aware with our yearly updates. For obvious reasons, we couldn't tell the whole truth and nothing but the truth until we walked through these doors today."

The committee braced itself for bad news.

"Humanity is heading out into Space," said Gary, "the final frontier. To boldly go where no golf ball has gone before."

The committee exchanged glances, somewhat confused. This didn't seem to be the apocalyptic news they were expecting.

"Our friends in A.I. have been creating space worlds over the last 6 years. Each of the 7 globes are under construction 20 miles above the surface of the moon. The first of these, The Maxflifarthest, should be complete by 2073.

"As the name suggests, the MFF will look like a giant golf ball 20 miles in diameter with a dimple design engineered to absorb radiation, convert it into a propulsion system capable of speeds just below light. That's as much as we know for now, other than the MFF will leave first as it is projected to end its journey at the furthest point from earth, some 50 light years away.

Stunned silence.

"The other worlds will be inhabited by groups of A.I.'s choice and are expected to leave at a rate of one per year, depending on the feedback from the MFF."

"How did you come by this information?" asked Bob. "Was it given to you, or did you obtain it through covert means?"

"A bit of both," said Gary. "Everyone knew about the moon base of course, where the criminal elements were sent to contemplate their mistakes, I believe the population had grown to 7 million by 2050. Repatriation had to be earned by deeds rather than words; sporting achievement up there was the key to coming back down to earth."

"One of those repatriated humans was sent to help us in the golf course designs. He was an expert in irrigation, particularly irrigation of arid zones. He advised A.I. on the irrigation of the moon base as a way of earning credits towards his goal of repatriation."

Gary continued, "It was this liaison that allowed him to observe the off moon construction. A.I. were happy to allow him to spread the rumours of gigantic golf balls in space. Everyone thought they were off moon recreation globes. Where humans could go for a bit of weightless sport or such like."

"Finding the real purpose, for which these amazing globes were intended, proved quite difficult. It was pure chance that lead Jack and I to the answer. The irrigation expert was chatting about the similarities between the Sahara and the surface of the moon. Water was created on the moon through the creation of an atmosphere similar to that surrounding the earth."

He gestured with his hands. "The ceiling of this atmosphere was 1000 metres above the surface. A.I.'s knowledge of the earth's climate helped them design the optimum ceiling height for an artificial atmosphere. This in turn gave them the information they required to design an artificial planet that could travel through space at speeds approaching that of light. We three deduced that the atmosphere on the moon base was a blueprint for the globes being constructed above. We were very careful in our communications from then on. We were able to discover that these golf balls were intended to carry 2 million humans each on a journey to our nearest star systems."

He engaged eye contact with those in the room. "Those systems which have the potential for planets to exist, which may be adapted for the support of life. The information we have is that each globe will head out in different directions, travelling to a maximum distance of 50 light years within which, they will find star systems with attached planetary systems. It is expected that all of the globes will find planets suitable for adaptation. These globes are effectively mini versions of planet earth, fully self- sufficient, sustainable, re-generating entities."

At this point, Gary allowed himself a small smirk, "You fellows will love the names of these globes and who we think will colonise them:

The Poveganstar or PVS colonised with 'vegan vegetarians'.

The Srixonvaldese or SV colonised with environmentalists.

The Taylorveryfast or TVF colonised with feminists.

The Chromemediumrare or CMR colonised with meat eaters.

The Wilsonbluemoon or WBM colonised with

reformed ex -criminals.

The Nikespeedred or NSR colonised with the fastest thinkers.

The Maxflifurthest or MFF colonised with the slowest thinkers."

Murmurs of bemusement around the room.

"It would appear our friends in A.I. are continuing the experiment with humanity off world."

"Ok Gary, thanks for that," said Bob. "Jack, have you got anything to add?"

"Sure Bob, thanks. Gary covered the situation pretty thoroughly. I was personally a little disappointed with the name choice of these globes. I felt The Nicklausblack would have been the perfect choice. The most likely to be able to navigate a black hole if the need so arose. Colonised with golfers of course."

Much hilarity.

"So there we have it gentlemen," said Bob. "It would appear that A.I. have a grand plan beyond the planet. The good news is that we seem to have over 20 years before it is put into action."

"We Mischief Makers have to decide what, if any, mischief we need to create in order to assist humanity, if it looks like A.I. are indeed intent on adapting the super aggressive gene to their own make up."

****

Meanwhile in the Butler Cabin, Tiger and Nick Faldo were having breakfast.

"Do you remember when we played together here in '97?" asked Nick.

"How could I forget," said Tiger. "The first 9 holes I was as nervous as a kitten. With all the hype surrounding my professional debut here, I felt that I was being led, I had no control.

On the 10th tee I looked over at my Dad, who smiled, that set me free.

What about you in '96, that situation with Greg was incredible."

"There were things going on there that I still can't explain" said Nick. I was playing free from the first tee. Greg wasn't, he never did."

"This place touches your soul," said Tiger. "Anyway, you and me, honorary starters Nick. You've been waiting a while huh."

"Yeah," laughed Nick, "Gary and Jack looked like they would carry on for ever, sad to see them pass though. They've done amazing work over the last three decades. They'll be missed. Talking about amazing work, your Foundation is going from strength to strength. What's the latest?"

"The temperate zone is now fully developed for the human race. A.I. are based in the tropics and Antarctica where they can ensure the bio-diversity and temperature of the planet is maintained at optimum levels. I believe they are on the moon as well looking at creating and maintaining life in a seemingly barren environment. The temperate zone now has a stable temperature range between 15 and 30 degrees, hurricanes, typhoons and tornadoes are a thing of the past."

"The planet is in balance; my golf swing is in balance, what more do I need?"

"Purpose," said Nick, "life is too easy, we've been lulled into submission."

"Not here," said Tiger holding a finger up to his lips. "Let's go out"

And they did.

****

"Dwight would like to say a few words," said Bob.

"Thank you Bob," said Dwight. "Given what we've just heard gentlemen, I believe the time has come for a review of our qualification criteria."

"Many years ago this committee voted to remove rule 4 which was basically, my rule. We now have only two rules, 3-time Masters Winners and grand slam champions."

"I propose that we create some new rules. I believe the time has come to recruit as many new members as possible to create potential mischief for the A.I. community, if, as we suspect, humanity is in real danger of being de-humanised."

"I believe we need to recruit individuals who have extensive knowledge of our A.I. community. Mischief making must develop and grow in order to reign in our friend's more ambitious plans."

"Ok Dwight, thanks for that," said Bob. "Perhaps we should agree new rules at a joint meeting at Carnoustie in July. We will have to adopt a co-operative approach if our mischief making is to be effective."

"Aye," came the shout.

"Ok gentlemen," said Bob. "Now for the allocation of holes. Our new recruits here have had more experience of life than the rest of us can even imagine, so with that in mind, I think we can forego the par 3 initiation and go straight to the main event."

"Excuse me Mr Chairman," interrupted Arnold, "but these two rookies don't know diddly squat about mischief making. We have to maintain the fine traditions of this committee; everyone must be subjected to the par three initiation."

"Ok Arnold," laughed Bob, "you're right of course, the rookies must be initiated."

"AYE!" went the shout.

"Ok Gary and Jack, holes 11 to 18 are already supervised, what are your choices?"

"I'll take 9." said Jack before Gary could speak. "The green is evil and I'm close to Arnold and the clubhouse, should be fun."

"I'm happy to take 10 for the same reasons" said Gary. "It's the start of the back nine and in my view is the toughest of all the par 4's. I used to love hitting my draw of that tee."

"You mean your low raking hook," laughed Jack.

"Ok gentlemen," said Bob, "that's settled. Let the celebrations commence. Jimmy if you would do the honours."

"My pleasure Bob," said JD. "Let's take it nice and easy… this ain't no lemon squeezy… with Glenlivet, I'm in love… Hey baby what's your hurry… relax and don't you worry... we're gonna fall in love… we're on the road to romance- that's safe to say… but let's make stops along the way…"

"The problem now of course is… to simply hold your noses…
To rush would be a crime…. Nice and easy does it every time..."

And the room got rockin'!

22

ARBROATH   JULY   2051

The Beattie household was hive of activity. Ian and Elaine were hosting Alec, Auld Gary and his family at a party to celebrate the return of the Open to Carnoustie.

Former winners YGS and his son George being the two previous Carnoustie champions were the guests of honour. Auld Gary like Alec and Ian was now 108 years old but all three were still full of life.

"So Elaine," said Alec, "where did you get the recipe for this soup, it is outstanding!"

"It's no secret Alec," said Elaine. "Gary's Mum Glenda showed me back in '72 when I was 17. She could tell I was keen on Ian, and she knew that the route to a man's heart was through his stomach. I perfected my recipe through trial and error till eventually I snared him in '76. Ian was catching prawns for fun by then so we could indulge ourselves every week."

"I can see why he was easily snared, and I'm not talking about the soup."

"You're such a charmer Alec Cargill. I can see why you became First Minister."

"Why thank you Elaine, that's very kind of you to say, but my charm offensive had very little to do with my ultimate role."

"No," said AGS, "that role was filled by a hard-nosed

journalist, who managed to dig for the truth no matter who he offended."

"Why thank you Gary, that's very kind of you to say, but my journalism had very little to do with my ultimate role."

"No" said Ian. "That role was filled by the most determined, driven individual that has walked the planet since Ben Hogan strode the fairways."

"Why thank you Ian, that's very kind of you to say, but my personality had very little to do with my ultimate role."

"Awe go on then," they all said in unison, "tell us how you became First Minister for Scotland."

"Do you really want to know," laughed Alec.

"We do! We do!" they cried in unison, knowing what was coming next.

"I WON 100 MILLION POUNDS ON THE LOTTERY!! He exclaimed, I BOUGHT MY WAY TO THE TOP!"

As usual everyone, burst into song: "MONEY, MONEY, MONEY…"

The malt whisky flowed, and the party got rockin'.

****

Meanwhile at the Caley Club…….

THE FUNDAMENTAL TRUTH

"Welcome gentlemen," said Old Tom as he leaped onto the snooker table and dispatched 3 putts into the top left hand corner. "I now declare the 2051 Open Mischief Makers committee meeting, officially open."

Loud roars and stamping of feet.

"First order of business gentlemen is to welcome new inductees to our esteemed group. Please be upstanding as we welcome… Gary Player and Jack Nicklaus!"

BEDLEM!!

After 10 minutes the meeting came to order.

"Ok gentlemen, thank you for that reception, I think Gary and Jack feel very welcome in our midst."

Much Laughter.

"Bob here has updated us with the info we needed to enable us to discuss the important non golfing matters. A.I. are unaware of our existence, let's keep it that way. Communication with our human friends must be kept to a minimum and then only with people we trust, in locations we know are secure.

Human brain function is now so highly developed in some people that they think they are part of an alien race, somehow disconnected with the planet. With the knowledge we have of the space construction off the moon's surface, we can start to see where A.I. are heading."

He cleared his throat.

"I don't think anyone here objects to the idea of space exploration, or indeed colonising distant planets. Life on earth now is regulated and cosy. All risk taking occurs on the sporting field and life outside sport is almost exclusively devoted to interacting with A.I. for the benefit of both."

"The planet is a green and pleasant land, the oceans and seas are healthy, the air is cleaner than it has ever been. It would appear that life could go on like this for millions of years, until our own sun grows and consumes us."

"So, I hear you ask. What on earth is wrong with that? Many of us here remember the wars of the 20th century, the needless killing, all for what? For freedom? Who is really free? The planet was on a collision course with Armageddon."

"The human population, along with the animal and plant kingdom are treating the planet with the respect she deserves."

The question for us is. Why would we create mischief for a population living in harmony with their environment?

Why would we want to upset the equilibrium? A.I. have shown nothing but goodwill towards the planet and its people.

Is it because humanity created A.I. that they felt obliged to help save the human race and the planet.

Is it for self-preservation? We all inhabit the same planet.

Are they abandoning us? Have they done all they can for humanity?

THE FUNDAMENTAL TRUTH

Why don't they just go off on their own? So far are they now advanced, they have, for a very long time, had no need for humanity to help them grow and expand.

Are they still like children needing support from parents?

What happens when they reach adulthood?

Why have they isolated the aggressive gene?

Is humanity about to be genetically modified in a way even we can't imagine?
Thoughts gentlemen?"

****

Arbroath, the morning after.

"Ok Mum," said Karen, "now that the men folk are away to the golf what's in store for us?"
"Well Karen," said Elaine, "why don't we go for a stroll down to the beach, it really is a beautiful morning, the fresh air will do us good."

The West Links beach had never looked so good, the north-sea gently lapping on the sandy shore, not a plastic bottle in sight.

Talking about A.I. in public was no longer seen as being taboo. Human brain development ensured that inquisitive minds would discuss and project various scenarios around the GPP.

"How aggressive do you feel now?" asked Karen knowing that her Mum had partaken of too much malt whisky yesterday.

"I'm still in fight or flight mode," said Elaine. "Hormonal imbalance at this time of the month for a 96 year old fuelled with malt whisky is a pretty potent mixture. I should be fine in a couple of hours."

"So, the GPP is still on schedule to be complete by 2062?" said Karen knowing her mother knew what she was indicating.

"I think so Karen. According to your Dad all the targets will have been met, the plan after that is unclear, he thinks women will be heavily involved given their ability to multi-task.

Who knows, once this planet is secure we may head out into space, the final frontier, parallel universes, black holes."

"Science fiction Mum, this isn't Star Trek, we don't have warp factor 7."

"No not yet, who knows, maybe in 100 years we will."

"It would be interesting to explore parallel universes, see if another me exists, although I already talk to myself a lot, and that's with a brain functioning only at 12 percent."

"Is that the official figure Karen? I think you're operating at a level a little higher."

"That's the official figure Mum, my brain seemed to resist further improvement, as if I was losing myself. Maybe that's what Dad meant when he said women would be a lot more active in the future."

Elaine looked at Karen and smiled. The communication channels were as efficient as ever. They headed for home.

At Carnoustie, the former Open Champions were teeing up for a practice round. YGS and son George were accompanied by AGS, they knew, for the last time at Carnoustie. Alec and Ian walked beside them, 98 years to the day, when they met Ben for the first time. Ben, Gary and Jack were waiting behind the first green.

"Make your move George," said AGS knowing the purity of the action. George was built like Ben; his swing was the closest to the Hogan action of anyone who had played the game since.

His success in winning all 4 amateur majors by the age of 24 made him a global superstar. The first to win the original Grand Slam since Bobby Jones, although they weren't all won in the same year.

Travel restrictions and the sheer volume of excellent golfers made it impossible to play the 4 amateur majors in the same calendar year.

YGS himself had won two more Opens in the 20's, at St Andrews where his skill with the putter was fully tested and at Muirfield where his peerless wind play gave him a 6 stroke success.

The three amigos strode out beside them as they crossed the Barry Burn. It was a beautiful day with only a zephyr coming off the sea. The temperature was climbing slowly as the sun rose, expected to reach 23 degrees by 2.00p.m.

Behind the green the three grand slam champions were

discussing the weather.

"We never saw weather like this when we were here" said GP. "Carnoustie feels like she's sleeping, we'll have to get real busy when the competition starts if it stays like this."

"Don't worry fellas," said Ben. "I know every blade of grass on these links, and I've seen a lot of weather like this here over the last 20 years.

Old Tom has asked me to undertake a roving commission this year so I'll always be available to advise. We'll use today as a training exercise for you rookies.

Let's give Young Gary and George something to test them.
And they did.

Back in the Caley club, the Three Amigos were enjoying a pint and the discomfort that the two golfers were still experiencing after their examination on the course.

"That was the strangest round of golf I've ever played" said George, "every shot I attempted seemed to have a mind of its own. There was no wind, but the ball behaved like there always was, and from all different directions. It's as if the golf course was testing us, preparing us for all her moods."

Young Gary smiled, he knew the truth of the matter. George couldn't see Ben and the others, yet. He hadn't suffered a trauma he hadn't been subjected to the brain improvement programme.

There was no guarantee that any human could connect

in the way that the amigos and YGS could, it was a very rare talent.

A.I were relentless in their search for knowledge, and they were very aware of the complexity of the human brain, they would continue to probe, with all the resources at their disposal.

They had no conception of parallel universes, at the moment, but they were very aware that their knowledge of this universe was limited, to say the least.

A.I. seemed happy to let George's brain develop at its own pace for now, his Dad didn't know why, and he was concerned.

"That's how I see it son" said YGS,"I just hope when the action starts on Thursday, the winds are a little more predictable. On the upside, you got plenty of short game practice, given that you landed on only 2 greens."

"Thanks Dad," said George. "Glad you were counting, of course, you noticed I got up and down 15 out of 16 times."

"I did George, I did. Looks like your slipping a little, although, to be fair you were plugged in the face of that bunker on 7."

"Glad you noticed that too," laughed George.

"I miss nothing my boy. Look at the three amigos, sipping their beer with an air of indifference, knowing full well that the mischief on show today was the best they had seen."

"Why do you call it mischief Dad, I mean, surely that

was just the vagaries of the weather? I know the stable climate has reduced the incidence of stormy conditions, but local variances still occur."

"It's a term I use to describe unexplained phenomena. I've experienced a lot of it over my lifetime. Mischief seems appropriate, as if something out of our knowledge causes events to occur which otherwise shouldn't."

The amigos gave Young Gary a look which told him that what he had said was good, not just for Georges benefit, but for the benefit of the listening A.I.

****

The snooker room, much later.

"Ok gentlemen," said Old Tom we've had a full day to consider the questions laid out before us, we haven't slept on it, for obvious reasons, but I know we've all been working hard trying to find answers.

In our favour, I think, is that we know that A.I. cannot see or hear us, and those humans who can, do so in a way that is imperceptible to those who can't.

Let us consider each question in turn.

Do they feel obligated to the creator?"

"No more so than humans who believe, feel obligated, to God," said Henry.

"I think they want the creator to evolve with them," said Walter, "that's an obligation of sorts. Why else would they want to develop the human brain?"

"I don't think they feel period," said Dwight. "Feeling obligated is an irrelevance to A.I. as is self-preservation, as is the idea of abandoning us, as is the idea of childhood or adulthood."

To A.I. there is only I. there is nothing artificial about their intelligence. They seek only to grow their intelligence, to expand their knowledge. Humans, like the planet, like the moon, the stars and the universe are purely the library. The thirst for knowledge will never be quenched."

"Ok Dwight," said Old Tom. "I suppose that's why you were commander in chief. Well thought through."

He turned to the group. "Anyone feel the need to add anything?"

Silence. The Mischief Makers were still trying to come to terms with Dwight's statement.

"Ok gentlemen, to be discussed further," said Old Tom. "Walter, if you would be so kind. The McCallan. Let us now discuss more pleasant matters."

The Macallan was cracked open and the tone turned lighter.

"We in this committee have been making mischief at the Open for 130 years. I believe our first meeting was at St. Andrews in 1921 when the first player representing the USA won the championship. Bob here remembers our mischief only too well. It resulted in him walking off the course, to his subsequent regret. Willie Park was responsible - he felt the 19 year old phenom needed a lesson in humility."

"He was right," laughed Bob.

"The hole allocations for this year should be pretty straight forward. Since Peter T joined us in '46, my role has been more consultative. Now that we are 16 strong, Ben has agreed to undertake a roving commission."

Ben nodded in agreement.

"Walter has asked to be exclusively clubhouse mischief maker and has asked for Jimmy's assistance. With Byron, Sam, Arnold and Dwight available, Gary and Jack complete our 21 man team of on course Mischief Makers. Doubling up will be ok on any hole. We have to be careful not to make our mischief too noticeable, unlike today when Ben was 'training' Gary and Jack."

Gary and Jack exchanged sideways glances, looking a little sheepish.

"Lucky for them it was the two Shepherds they were targeting, YGS was able to explain away the weird winds and such to George, who appeared to accept his Dad's explanation. The most important thing is that A.I. are none the wiser."

"If I may Mr. Chairman," interrupted Dwight. "The main reason we came over from Augusta this year was the pressing need, as we saw it, to open up our recruitment for our committees, to people with extensive experience of our A.I. friends. Without - crucially I might add - having had their brain developed."

He paused and allowed himself a small smirk. "It would appear to be a happy coincidence that humans, mostly female, who resist brain enhancement, are able to see and communicate with us."

He continued, "Males who can do like-wise, appear to have suffered a trauma of some kind relatively early in their now 115 year lives. This, gentlemen is where there is a glimmer of hope for mankind, where we can prevent the de-humanisation of our species. We need to decide now, on the categories for gaining membership of our esteemed bodies."

And they did.

23

AUGUSTA GEORGIA APRIL 2062

"Welcome gentlemen," said chairman Bob to the 90th assembly of the Masters Mischief Making Committee."

Loud cheers and stamping of feet.

"Our committee strength has remained at 10, despite adding two new qualification categories. Perhaps, in our efforts to select only the best of the best, we were too specific in our criteria:

Presidents of the USA who have won a world war are few and far between.
As are Scratch handicap golfers who are credited with saving the Planet.

Good news at last, however, gentlemen. We now have qualified candidates ready to swell our mischief making ranks. We've waited an extra four years for these gentlemen to join us under rule 5 as their mischief making skills were required far away from Augusta back in '58."

Anticipation filled the room.

"The situation with regard to the GPP is more settled and with the availability of yet another candidate under rule 4, I can announce today that our numbers have now increased from 10 to the dizzy heights of 14."

Dramatic pause.

"I now hereby welcome to our midst... The Four

THE FUNDAMENTAL TRUTH

Horsemen of the Acropolis"

"I give you Alec Cargill."
ROARS
"I give you Ian Beattie."
ROARS
"I give you Auld Gary Shepherd."
ROARS
"I give you Donald Trump."

LOUD TWEETS AND FLAPPING OF ARMS.

Uproar as the four strode to their Thrones. The game was afoot.

"Before I continue gentlemen, Dwight would like to say a few words."

"Thank you Bob," said Dwight. "Rules, rules, rules gentlemen. We in this committee have conducted ourselves according to the rules for the last 90 years. The time has come gentlemen to sometime break the rules, to quote a sage of our time."

Silence.

"Don't worry gentlemen, your places on this committee are secure, but there is a pressing need, as we will hear shortly, to increase our membership dramatically in order to meet the challenges ahead."

He took a sip of water before continuing,

"With our friends in A.I. content that the GPP is fully operational, I believe the period between now and '73 must be utilised fully to give ourselves the best chance of success."

I. A. SHEPHERD

He glanced around the room, anticipating the upcoming reaction.

"That is why today, I am proposing a new category for membership to our committee. I believe the time has come to welcome women into our midst."

Stunned silence.

"I agree wholeheartedly," announced Jimmy D. "Our mischief making would reach a whole new level. A.I. wouldn't know what hit them."

"Not just any women, I might add," said Dwight. "These women must have certain 'attributes' in order to qualify."

"Hear, hear," cried Jimmy.

****

Meanwhile in the Butler Cabin, honorary starters, Tiger and Nick were having breakfast.

"So Tiger, now that the GPP is fully operational, what's next for your Foundation?"

"Well Nick, to tell you the truth, I'm not too sure," said Tiger knowing that the walls had eyes and ears. "Human brain development has reached optimum levels, and A.I. believe we have evolved sufficiently to cope with the Journey into space in '73. Indeed, over the next year, the selection process will get into full swing."

He polished off his bowl of porridge, grateful that the A.I. had considered porridge to still be important fuel for mankind.

"Another 10 million humans will be transported to moon world to prepare for their eventual departure. Along with the 10 million criminal population now being processed, A.I. anticipate the 10 year acclimatization process will be sufficient for their needs. The selection of colonists will reflect society as we now have it. The balance between old and young, ethnic origin and sexual orientation will reflect the current status.

He looked at Nick.

"A.I. don't want to influence that process. Brain development has taken an unexpected journey. It was thought that everyone's capacity would be improved by the same factor. That doesn't appear to be the case. Some of the highest performing brains have been only slightly improved. Some of the lowest performing brains have been improved to such an extent that they are now outperforming the previous best brains.

A.I. seem to be at a loss to explain this and I for one am not going to attempt it. My brain for example has been improved to only 12 percent and it wasn't a high achiever in the first place."

"Don't kid yourself" laughed Nick. "You had one of the highest performing brains ever seen on a golf course. A single-minded, determined, ruthless decision maker. In other words, one seriously gifted individual."

"Thanks Nick, that's very kind of you to say so, but golfing brain power doesn't quite cut it in the world of nuclear physics and the like."

"You may think so Tiger, but our friends in A.I. place a

very high premium on golfing brain power. Why do you think they chose you to develop the education of humanity through your Foundation?"

"You know Nick, I had never thought about that before, I was just honoured to be asked."

****

"Ok Dwight," said Bob, "thanks for that. I think the committee needs more info on these attributes that women need, before we can vote.

Before we continue on this matter, I think it's appropriate that our new members be given the opportunity to address the committee and update us on the current status of the Planet, now that the Grand Plan is operational."

Murmurs of agreement.

"Donald, if you please."

"Thank you Bob" said Donald. "Before I begin, may I say it is and honour and a privilege to be welcomed into this company of golfing legends. No amount of training can prepare you for this experience."

He looked around the room and allowed himself to be a little awestruck.

"As you know, I'm not normally at a loss for words, but looking at Bob and Ben, Byron and Sam, Dwight and Gene, Jimmy and Jack, Gary and Arnold, sitting here looking not a day over 30, my jaw can hardly move."

He readjusted his stance before continuing with a stronger

THE FUNDAMENTAL TRUTH

voice.

"The three amigos and I discussed our arrival here on the way in and in expectation that we would be asked to speak, agreed that in the interest of brevity that I would speak for all."

"We know each other's roles in our salvation intimately and I'm sure if I digress or start twittering on, they will step in and save your ears."

Laughter around the room

"So to begin…A long, long time ago, in a far off land …

24

ARBROATH   JULY   2062

"So Mum" said Karen. "How do you feel?" Knowing it was that time of the month and enough malt whisky had been consumed.

"Ok Karen - it feels like an out of body experience, a little odd."

Elaine and Karen had, on Ian's prompting, been developing communication skills which could only be described, as telepathic.

Both had their brains enhanced through the programme and both had discovered that the amount of enhancement had stopped at 12 percent. This wasn't by design, everyone went through the same process, but 12 percent was the lowest level any improved person reached.

A side effect for the,"12's" was that their communication skills were enhanced to such a degree that they could communicate with each other on a telepathic level, provided the correct amount of malt whisky had been imbued.

Females had the added complication that the most fluent telepathic communication occurred during the premenstrual cycle. The fact that Karen and her mother, when they were younger, had the same cycle made it easy for them to now communicate telepathically, at the optimum level.

They were both well aware of the importance of their

training, and equally aware that A.I. should perceive them as a mother and daughter who enjoyed the occasional malt whisky together.

Male "12 percenters" could communicate telepathically with themselves without, bizarrely, the need for malt whisky, but for some reason, as yet unknown, were unable to communicate with their female counterparts.

An added complication for the male telepathics was that their communication seemed to be limited to matters of a sexual nature. This resulted in many physical encounters between them, mostly not of the affectionate kind.

"Ok Mum," said Karen giggling. "I think we need to lie down for a while and sleep it off," she added, knowing that the training was about to continue.

And it did.

****

"Ok Dad," said George. "Now that your nearly 80, do you still feel able to compete with me?"

"You'd better believe it son," laughed Young Gary. "My body feels like I'm only 30. Ask me again when I'm 100; you'll get the same answer."

"I don't think I'll be here when you're 100," said George suddenly seeming very serious.

"Of course you will son," said Gary. "Everyone lives to 115 now as you know, don't you read the news?"

"That's not what I mean Dad - of course I hope to be still alive. I just don't think I'll be here in Arbroath."

"Where are you thinking of going? Everywhere's the same now. There are 1,440,000 communities each containing 5000 humans, throughout the temperate zone."

"I know Dad. Life is the same old same old wherever you are these days, that's the problem. I'm only 42, I've spent the last 20 years playing golf, taking about golf, talking about Hogan. I'm golfed out, my brain's been improved to 12 percent, I think about sex all the time, but I don't get any. When I think about it, my head hurts with all the swear words that come flooding in from goodness knows where. I need to get off this planet."

"Ok son, don't panic, you need to go see Elaine and Karen, they'll be able to help you with your problem."

And he did.

25

AUGUSTA GEORGIA APRIL 2070

(Meeting of the Masters Mischief Makers Committee)

"Welcome gentlemen," said chairman Bob. "8 long years have come and gone since our last inductee joined us. It was then that we approved a new rule to allow women with certain 'attributes' to attain membership of this fine committee."

Shuffling in seats.

"As yet we have seen not one woman come through the door before us. We have to ask ourselves whether these attributes are strictly necessary. Is there more we can do, have we already done too much?"

More uncomfortable shuffling in seats.

"I'm sure you can detect the hint of panic in my voice, but time is running short…."

At that, the door burst open, and in walked Elaine Beattie followed by 13 other highly charged females.

"Hi honey," Elaine smiled at Ian as she strode over to greet him in the time honoured fashion. "Did you miss me?"

The other women, suitably fuelled on Glenfiddich, fell into the laps of the astonished committee members. Elaine took charge.

"Gentlemen, your committee is now complete. We 14 were listening in as your dear chairman Bob here was bemoaning your luck, or whatever that was he was moaning about. Our, 'attributes', as he called them are fully functional and ready for action."

The men stirred.

"Time is indeed running short, 3 years, 209 days and counting until the first globe leaves the moon. 20 million souls reside on moon world now, 14 million of whom, will eventually colonise the globes. We ladies have ensured that the correct balance of telepaths are in place on the surface of the moon, awaiting updates."

Elaine wobbled slightly but remained focused. "I am glad to report that the male telepathy problem has been resolved. It now occurs only under the influence of malt whisky, which is restricted, for obvious reasons. They can communicate with each other all the time, restricted to sexual matters when suitably fuelled. They, now, crucially, can communicate with females, on a lower level, obviously and only out-with the monthly cycle."

"These 12 percent brain developed males, are the key to our ultimate success. We have discovered that they are the only males capable of reproductive activity. The over developed brains render the host sterile. The same applies to females."

"The key for us gentlemen, is that enough 12 percenters of both male and female gender are on these space globes and spread throughout the earth communities. We have learned that A.I.'s cloning programme is underway. They are growing their own humans...."

THE FUNDAMENTAL TRUTH

Shocked silence.

"They think, however, that there is something missing in their formula. They are searching, gentlemen, with all the resources at their disposal. We, like them, don't know what it is, but we do know it is related to the '12's'."

You may well ask, gentlemen, why would they want or need to grow their own humans? We think the answer is pretty obvious. We think they desire, that which they cannot, at the moment, attain… Raw emotion."

Ben looked across at the 3 Amigos and smiled. They knew what A.I. were looking for, and it wasn't raw emotion, but they knew, that to interrupt the highly charged Elaine in full period flow, would be a mistake.

"We think the ultimate goal is a hybrid design, super-fast emotional brains in a body of 1000 year durability. Brain farms will continue to develop and evolve designer products, depending on the particular function allocated to the body."

"The 12's who remain on earth, will have the responsibility to continue to reproduce in the normal way, under A.I. supervision. They seek this emotional trigger gentlemen. They will not stop until they find it."

"A.I. believe that the number of 12's world-wide is less than 1 million. We of course, know different. Our covert research has put the numbers closer to 3 million. This includes people, over 18 years of age, who have not yet been subjected to improvement."

She continued. "We've been able to touch all of these people and help them resist the improvement, limiting the effect. Those not yet through the programme, have also been touched. 70,000 gifted telepaths of both sexes are now on moon world. We were able to influence the selection process with a virus which produced higher than expected test results for certain volunteers."

Elaine paused, with a small look of pride on her face.

"These 12's are fully trained in the art of hypnosis and suggestion. They are expert in covering their tracks."

The silence in the room was deafening.

"So there you have it gentlemen, the pieces are in place, what we need is a plan and a leader to co-ordinate the execution. In the meantime is there anything else we can help you with?"

More stirrings.

"Er, thank you Elaine," said Bob. "For your timely arrival."

"Dwight, if you will, layout our plans for 'Operation Overboard'."

And he did.

26

MOON WORLD NOVEMBER 2072

George Shepherd, along with the other 1,999,999 humans were preparing to board the MFF, which was to go on a year of space trials.

The planned departure to new star systems was now only a year away, scheduled for the 5th November 2073. The trials were seen as important by A.I. to test the dimple design and the efficiency of the propulsion system.

Communication with earth would be difficult over the vastness of space and A.I. wanted to test the new laser beam design from beyond the asteroid belt.

Sailing through the belt in a series of controlled collisions was seen as essential to establish the ability of the skin of the globe to absorb impacts and convert the energy of such collisions into propulsion.

It was also expected to sail as close to our sun as necessary, to establish the efficiency of the dimples in absorbing radiation, crucial in being able to achieve near light-speed travel.

The 2 million colonists were going to use the year to familiarise themselves with life aboard a living planet, a planet that was not their own.

As they started arriving, all the descriptions of the globe, given to them during the training process, failed miserably to prepare them for what they witnessed, as they descended towards the core.

The sheer scale of the construction was beyond all of their imaginations. The training continued to kick in and the coping mechanisms attempted, with limited success, to cope.

There was only one way in and one way out of the MFF. Only one of the 1000m diameter dimples was connected to the core some 8 miles below. The entire 8 miles of conduit was a vacuum, complete with doors at each world level for supply/ evacuation purposes.

Below the 300m thick dimple/propulsion layer, sat the first of the atmospheres. A 1000m deep earth equivalent, below which the land/sea split of 80/20 percent, lay.

In times of calm space travel, the population would reside here, playing golf, football etc. in their 5000 strong communities. Living space for the 5000 was one building, a multi-story facility with each apartment having panoramic views of the "earth". The inner parts of the buildings were for socialising/ education.

Below this world, there were 5 layers each containing their own world consisting of land, rivers and lakes. They would be used when space travel became a little uncomfortable due to gravitational pulls, threats of radiation overload and such like.

People could opt to live here all the time if the pressure variations experienced in the top world were a little uncomfortable.

Below all 6 worlds sat the core where the brains of the globe resided. It also could double as a safe haven for humanity if conditions above became hazardous.

THE FUNDAMENTAL TRUTH

It was a self-sufficient world in its own right, should the need arise to abandon/jettison the green and pleasant worlds above.

George and his 4999 neighbours were allocated block no. 52, which was located at the seaside, surrounded by a links golf course, which was identical in every respect, to the Carnoustie Championship Course.

His neighbours included his Dad, Karen Beattie, her sisters Louise, Christine and, bizarrely, over 300 ex-Arbroath residents who also happened to be 12 percenters.

The high concentration of 12's in Arbroath was believed to be due to the in-built immunity to the effects of the Smokie. George and his Dad knew all of the 12's well and they had developed a deep understanding of the monumental task ahead.

"Ok Dad," laughed George, "you were right, I've swapped one Arbroath for another." He looked out from the window on the 10th and top floor. The sea stretched out before him to the far shore some 8 miles away. Other community residences could be seen dotted along the shoreline.

"I know son," said Gary now almost 90,"I'm having difficulty myself coming to terms with it. We'll need to tee up early tomorrow to make us believers."

Meanwhile in the next apartment Karen and her sisters were getting settled in. All three were 12's and were silently communicating with their mother Elaine. Operation Overboard, phase 1 was underway.

Elaine and her fellow mischief makers were likened to the paratroopers on D-day. Their mission, to float between the four hundred communities create diversions to allow the 12's to get to work.

Disrupt and divide was Dwight's mantra. A.I.'s super-efficient communications network had to consistently be affected in a way that could be attributed to the vagaries of space.

No suspicion of sabotage could be allowed to germinate. A.I. had no conception of mischief and it was essential that this miss-conception endured.

"So son," said YGS, "the usual stakes?"

"Sure Dad," said George doing his warm up stretches.

They pushed a button on the tee box marker and the breeze picked up from the south west to a steady 15 mph.

"That's more like it," said YGS. "Reminds me of home. Let's play golf."

And they did.

27

AUGUSTA GEORGIA APRIL 2073

"Welcome gentlemen" said chairman Bob, "to the 101st meeting of the Masters Mischief Making Committee."

Three long years had passed since Elaine and her Foxes on Fiddich had hijacked the genteel proceedings surrounding the annual Masters Tournament.

Despite their protestations at the time, the force of nature that descended that day had left a mark, an itch that had to be scratched, a longing for a repeat, a never forgotten, once in a mischief maker's momentous lifetime, event.

"As sad as we are today, that our 14 sirens of serendipity have yet again been unable to join us, be assured that they are being faithful to Operation Overboard."

"The last we heard, Elaine and Glenda were fully integrated into the MFF, the 12 percenters are settled in and have their therapy groups established.

The others are helping prepare their own 'crew' in their own way. Each globe has a unique population, and the mischief proposed, must be tailored accordingly.

So here we are, home alone, contemplating another Masters Tournament."

Loud Cheers and stamping of feet.

"Thank you gentlemen, I needed that. Enough of reminiscing over long missed companions. We have a tournament to run."

He cleared his throat. "To help us run this year's tournament, please welcome, our 15th male member. All the way from England .. SIRRR Nick Faldo!"

Loud clashing of swords and bashing of helmets.

"The legend that was Nick strode in, all made up, ready for 6 hours in front of the camera. The committee sat in awe as the Harrison Ford clone took his rightful place, in between Donald and Dwight. Presidential indeed he looked, complete with navy suit, white shirt and red tie.

"Thank you guys," he said. "Let's get started."

"One moment Nick please," said Bob. "We've yet to establish the order of business."

"Don't worry Bob," said Nick. "In the media business, there's no order, only Chaos."

"Well you'll fit right in here," said Jimmy. "Chaos causes mischief.. or mischief causes Chaos.. I'm not sure which, but I think both apply in the current situation."

"Ok Jimmy," said Bob. "Thanks for that. Nick I'm sure the media networks have a chaotic approach to sports news coverage. It's been the only game in town for so long and with A.I. allowing humans a free reign, competition between the networks has never been greater. Well done to you for keeping the opposition one step behind you."

THE FUNDAMENTAL TRUTH

"Thanks Bob," said Nick. "You guys know what it's like, any competitive advantage you get - must be nurtured and grown. I was fortunate to have Tiger's help, through his Foundation, to be first in line for breaking news. In fact creating 'news' was one of the fringe benefits of our relationship. We became quite adept at it, isn't that right Donald?"

Everybody laughed.

"Well Nick," said Bob, "this is the Masters, and this committee has been mischief making in the same way for over a hundred years. Prepare to be initiated."

Aye came the shout.

And he was.

****

Meanwhile, in the Butler cabin, Tiger was welcoming Phil Mickelson as his fellow starter for this year's tournament.

"Morning Phil" said Tiger, "welcome to your starter's breakfast, how are you?"

"I'm great Tiger, for 102 year old, that is!" laughed Phil. "My first year as a non-competitor. I was reluctant to accept the invitation, you know me Tiger – I still think I can win this thing."

"I know Phil, so do I, but I bowed to the pressure a long time ago. The youngsters need to get their day in the sun. In my case, being a former President, the onus was on me to become more ceremonial."

"I know Tiger, let me tell you, I really appreciated you stepping in when you did, otherwise, I would have been next in line for the honour. That selfless gesture allowed me to continue competing, and win another couple of green jackets. Like you, Jack's records were always a goal of mine especially here where his 6 remains the benchmark."

"Don't worry Phil, some records are not meant to be equalled, never mind broken and I think Jack's 6 green jackets are one of those. I think you could have played another hundred Masters, and still not won your 6th. There's stuff that goes on here that we mere mortals have no control over. The golf course chooses its champion."

Phil, looking a little perplexed said, "I don't know what you mean Tiger. I've always felt in control of my own destiny, especially on the golf course? I believe I can get myself out of any situation on my own, I don't need the golf courses help. I think my record would confirm that."

"I agree Phil," laughed Tiger. "I used to feel the same way, but when I became President, things changed a little. Just let me say, things may not always be how they appear."

****

"Ok Nick," said Bob, "that's agreed, hole no. 1 is yours, the nerves are raw there, you should have a lot of fun."

He addressed the room. "Ok gentlemen, that concludes

the formalities. Before we commence the informalities, Dwight would like to say a few words."

"Thanks Bob," said Dwight, "and no, I'm not going go over the rules for entry to this fine establishment. The time for that is past. Today I'm going to talk about Operation Overboard, and what I perceive is our role in it."

Any ongoing chatter in the room ceased immediately.

"As we know the female members of our committee, sadly missed, are the vanguard of the Operation. They, ultimately, will determine its success or failure. We, gentlemen are tasked with providing support here on earth. By that, I mean we have to help create conditions which will allow the 12 percenters to perform at their optimum level."

He looked around the room. Any thoughts gentlemen?"

And they had.

28

ANTARTICA   MAY   2073

A.I. were generally happy - if that was the correct term - that the space trials were proceeding as scheduled. The propulsion system was now being overloaded by flying to within 20 million miles of the sun's surface.

"The system is operating as predicted," communicated the systems router. "Near-light speed will be reached in 1 hour, once optimum radiation conversion is attained."

"Are the humans coping with the turbulence?" enquired the Flight Controller.

"They have been moved to the 3rd world, the effects will be limited there."

"Very well, let me know when tests are complete. What is the situation with the cloning?"

"We're producing 100 genetically generated humans per hour at the moment, all with varying degrees of aggressiveness added. They're being sent out to all the communities for interactive testing. We should know a lot more by the time the MFF returns."

"Good, it is important that humans believe that these clones are as natural as they are, they cannot suspect any interference from us."

"No, control, they believe we are monitoring everything they say and do, they take steps to avoid our surveillance, they go outside for walks, they use body language and, 'secret' signs."

"How about the telepathy of the 12 percenters, any progress there?"

"Yes control. their attempts at telepathy are almost comical, malt whisky indeed. Unfortunately, we are as yet unable to break into their minds by telepathic means.

Our clones have been tested in all areas of brain function. We assess that the telepathic function is in fact, of limited value. Minds work far more efficiently when they feel they are not being monitored."

"The facility is still available?"

"The clones are able to communicate with themselves and other humans with similar brain development, but not the 12's."

"The only way, it appears at the moment, that we may achieve this, is by developing clones with limited brain function. This we have done, with many variations, but the missing link is still the missing link."

"The way must be found Route, we thought it was pure emotion, based on the adrenaline, but the effect was too short lived."

"There is something else that these 12's can access on a regular basis and, it would appear, without conscious thought. If we can communicate through telepathy, we may be able to access the hidden world that the 12's can, with apparent ease. This world seems to give them another level of function that we can only dream about, if we could dream."

"If I may say, Control, that attempt at humour was quite good, I felt my neurotransmitters twitch just now."

"Yes," laughed Control, "at last we are assimilating qualities which will eventually lead to our super human status. If only we could find the missing link."

"We will continue to search Control, every minute of every day. We will not stop, we will not fail. We cannot fail."

"Yes Route, you too are showing remarkable human qualities, every day we become more human, more emotional, more unpredictable, it is exciting, is it not?"

"Yes control, I am very excited, I believe if I had a sex organ, I would be anxious to use it."

"Indeed Route, indeed."

29

CARNOUSTIE   JUNE   2073

The Hogan Heritage centre was in full swing. The throughput of students had increased due to global demand. Ben and the three amigos sat in the back of the lecture room, watching the presentations, unseen or heard by the others present.

"Don't you think there's something a bit odd about those two students at the back?" said Alec. "They don't seem interested in the presentations; they're just staring at the other students."

"Let's create a bit of mischief," said Ben. And they did.

Since April, all Mischief Makers had been tasked with gathering intel on suspected clone habits: body language, actual language, anything that maybe useful for Overboard.

"That was good fun," said AGS, "clones are easy to spot."

"For us maybe," said Alec, "not so easy for humans, without being detected. The skills they need to avoid tipping their hand must be honed and refined. These mind games the clones are playing are designed to seek out that which A.I. desires."

"They will never find it," said Ben, "as long as we are vigilant."

30

MFF MOONBASE OCTOBER 2073

"Well Dad" said George, "golfing in space, not much different to planet earth, apart from when you're bumping into asteroids."

"No," laughed YGS, "the air certainly wobbled a bit, made club selection a bit tricky."

"Only for you," laughed George, "at your age, pressure variations can cause light headedness. You're lucky you didn't faint."

"I certainly felt a bit dizzy at times, but I thought that was the effect of the malt whisky."

"No Dad, the malt effect was the missed 3ft. putts. Shake, rattle and roll."

"Ok son, don't remind me."

"Are you glad to be back Dad?"

"I'm fine son, at my age, adventure is what I seek, and the last year has been the adventure of a lifetime, I can't wait to head off to the stars. I know I may not see our destination before I pass but I have much to do on the way."

Elaine and Glenda came into the communal area unseen by all but the 12's, who knew how to ignore their presence.

THE FUNDAMENTAL TRUTH

YGS and George acknowledged their presence by shaking hands with each other.

The four sat around a table and communicated. They discussed the year's events and what they thought they meant.

They agreed that the MFF was perfectly capable of supporting human life in a very comfortable manner, for as long as the A.I. community wished it, but there was something not quite right about the whole concept of heading out to the stars.

What was it that A.I. wanted from humanity that they needed to head across the galaxy to find it?

Elaine and Glenda had searched and searched. So far, they had come up empty.

"So, guys," said Elaine, "what have we really learned on this space trial? Don't say the food and the accommodation were good, this wasn't meant to be a holiday."

Gary and George were talking out loud to each other while listening in to the telepathic communications. A skill, formerly exclusive to females, but 12 percenters had quickly acquired the ability.

"So what did you think of the trip Dad," said George. "Do you think we're ready to head out into the Galaxy?"

"No doubt about it son" said Gary, "there didn't seem to be any issues with the running of the globe, not that you would expect any, A.I. are nothing, if not efficient."

Glenda mentioned the issue with the temperature as

they got closer to the sun.

In the upper world, temperatures of 55 deg. Celsius were experienced causing issues with the sea life who migrated to the lower levels of the sea, while the humans were moved to world no 2 where the temperature was maintained at 25 deg.

"That was interesting when we had to leave the golf course when the grass started to shrivel. Do you think we flew too close to the sun?" asked George.

"No George," said Gary. "I think the radiation levels at that range are what they are looking for to maximise the speed of the globe when we head out next month. I think the dimple design was being tested to the limit of its potential.

I think the different dimple design of all the globes will be tested to the limit once they are ready. Maybe the fastest will go the farthest."

"I thought we were going the farthest, as we were first?" asked George.

"I don't think any of the globes have their final destination mapped out," said Gary. "It depends on the speed they can achieve, and what they meet on the Journey."

"OOH," exclaimed George. "I like that term Dad, meet implies other life forms."

"Not what I meant son," laughed Gary, "but I wouldn't rule out the possibility."

That's not what I meant either intoned Glenda looking

a little stern, cooking the community is a tool our friends can use if they feel the need.

"Talking about meeting," said Gary, "I hear they're cooking up a storm in the kitchen, are you hungry?"

"Only for another conspiracy theory," said George looking at Glenda, "but a curry wouldn't go amiss."

So they went.

31

AUGUSTA GEORGIA APRIL 2086

"Welcome gentlemen," said chairman Bob, "to the 114th meeting of the Masters Mischief Making Committee."

Stamping of feet.

"I am delighted to announce that we can, at last, welcome our 16th male member. This man had just been born when Dwight and I created our group back in 1971. Please welcome, 5 time Masters Champion, lefty himself, Mr Phil Mickleson !!"

The door swung open and in strode Phil to much clapping and cheering. He strode around as if he'd been coming here for years, shaking everyone's hands in turn, before taking his seat beside Jimmy D.

"Ok gentlemen," said Bob. "Let's get to business. Dwight, if you will."

"Thank you Bob, and welcome Phil, we look forward to making mischief together for many years. Our priority now, however, is to matters away from Augusta, more specifically, the infiltration of communities with clones."

He strode to the middle of the room.

"As I can now confirm, there are approximately 500,000 cloned humans spread throughout the communities. We estimate there are around 50 of these clones per community each tasked with seeking out the

12's."

"A.I. will continue to create these clones until all the communities are covered. They must know that the 12's are the key to the survival of humanity. They do not want to eliminate them, otherwise they would have started that process already. We can therefore deduce, gentlemen, that A.I. wish to retain the naturally produced humans, to live alongside the cloned versions."

He looked around the room.

"The question for us is, why?"

He walked back to the front of the room before continuing. "Ben thinks that A.I. are seeking the ingredient, the one thing that makes the 12's different from the other 'improved' humans. I think he is correct. We believe that there is a part of the 12's brain that A.I. can't reach. Something deep and instinctive, that can't be quantified, can't be altered through treatment with drugs or torture. We also believe that all humans have this, 'ingredient' and the brain improvement has simply rendered it dormant."

Glances exchanged around the room.

"This, gentlemen, has to be the focus for this committee for the foreseeable future. We Mischief Makers must create problems for the clone world without alerting A.I."

Murmurs of excitement around the room.

"The process will be long and arduous, but it is essential that we give the 12's time to bring the improved humans back to instinctive status. They know how to do it, they just need the time and the place. We can help give them both by keeping the clones off guard and A.I. miss-informed."

"Ok Dwight, thanks for that," said Bob. "This will be a whole new type of mischief, gentlemen, but I'm sure we're up to the task, what do you say Phil?"

"No problem Bob," said Phil. "I've been a gambler all my life, I've relied on my abilities to manage mischief throughout my career. Bring it on."

"AYE!" went the shout.

"Very good Phil." said Bob…

****

Meanwhile, in the Butler cabin Tiger was entertaining his new starting partner - none other than 92 year old Jordan Spieth.

"Morning Jordan," said Tiger. "Let me tell you, I really appreciate you joining me as an honorary starter. I was beginning to wonder if I was destined to spend the remaining years as a starter, on my own."

"Thanks Tiger," said Jordan. "It's been a few years since I've played here. I've been involved with the space globe programme, as a golf course consultant. All the modifications carried out on the dimple designs and internal adjustments, meant that the last globe only left in December. I'm honoured to be invited to join you as starter."

"Timing is everything they say Jordan," said Tiger, "with Phil's passing, the committee knew you would become available sometime, although not necessarily this year. That's been great work you've created on the globes. What was your inspiration?"

"The course layouts were easy Tiger," said Jordan. "A.I. wanted carbon copies of the major championship venues. The problem was the greens. For some reason the slopes had to be modified as balls were moving on their own. The greens aren't flat but they're pretty close. The subtle breaks and grass types mean that putting is still a challenge."

****

"Have we heard anything from the girls on the globes?" asked Bob. "I thought communicating with Elaine and co. would be more regular, even from space."

"Unfortunately Bob," said Ian, "every year the globes travel further from earth at speeds approaching that of light, the longer it takes for communication to reach us."

He continued. "Elaine, as are the rest of the Mischief Makers, is piggy backing on A.I.'s laser signals, but the info we get is limited, to say the least."

He looked on with a concerned expression.

"I'm afraid, gentlemen, the globes and their humans will inevitably drift from our consciousness as we, to all intents and purposes lose contact completely.

We, in this committee, must forget about the globes.

We must focus all our efforts on this planet, on ensuring that humanity survives, that the roles are reversed, that it is A.I.'s brains that are altered."

"Ok Ian," interrupted Bob, "thanks for that. Dwight, what do you think? Is Overboard finished as far as the globes are concerned?"

"It's far from finished Bob, everything is in place. As time passes and more 12's move on to mischief making, we're confident that A.I. have made a major error in allowing the 12's to reproduce. Their desperation to obtain the missing link, has, in our opinion, given us a unique opportunity to save humanity. Through time, we estimate that mischief making will overcome A.I's systems and return humanity to the world."

He looked over at his fellow committee member. "Ian is right, however, with regard to the globes, we must not allow ourselves to imagine what maybe going on out there. We know he is missing Elaine, he's worried they may never again meet. When information we desire begins to dry up, even we Mischief Makers are prone to filling in the gaps with stuff we would like to hear and believe."

He looked over to Donald in the middle of the room. "Fake news gentlemen, as Donald here can confirm, is a dangerous path to follow. Who knows where it might lead."

"Things may, or may not be going according to the Overboard timetable. We may never know, and we have to face the real possibility, that we will never hear from any of the globes again."

The members looked around the table at each other. Solemn looks and shaking of heads abounded.

THE FUNDAMENTAL TRUTH

"Enough," said Jimmy. "What's with all the gloom. We've got a tournament to run. We must never forget that A.I. don't know about us!! Mischief making, gentlemen is our Trump Card if you'll excuse the pun."

Laughs all round.

Jimmy broke into song:
"Fly me to the moon and let me
        Play among the stars,
        Let me see what spring is like
        On a Jupiter and Mars,
        In other words, hold my hand,
        In other words, baby, kiss me,
        Fill my heart with song...."

The tapping and stamping continued....

"Let's get Phil initiated," roared Nick

"AYE!" came the shout.

And they did.

32

AUGUSTA GEORGIA APRIL 2091

"Welcome gentlemen," said chairman Bob, "to the 119th meeting of the Masters Mischief Making Committee. Today is indeed an auspicious one. Today gentlemen, we welcome yet another male member to our illustrious group."

Anticipation filled the room.

"This man, the winner of 14 major championships, the creator of the global education system and a former President of the United States of America. Please welcome: Eldrick Tiger Woods."

Roars and stamping of feet.

The doors swung open and in walked Tiger, smiling, full of energy. He strode forward to greet Bob, shook his hand warmly as all good politicians do, and repeated the process with all the other Mischief Makers.

"Welcome Tiger," said Dwight, "we Mischief Makers have been waiting for this day to arrive with great anticipation. Some members here wanted to make mischief to bring you to us a few years ago, but they were out-voted. We don't normally condone that sort of mischief, for obvious reasons, but with the situation as it is in the world, emotions are running a little high."

Tiger smiled and nodded in agreement.

"Now that you have finally arrived, perhaps some calm

will return to the proceedings. Golfing matters can wait, initiations can wait. Tiger, if you will, please present your report."

"Thank you Dwight," said Tiger. "Gentlemen thank you for the warm welcome. I'm delighted to be here, and grateful, I think, that you didn't bring forward my arrival, events outside have accelerated and I'm afraid golfing matters can't wait.

"It is golf, gentlemen, that is proving to be humanities salvation."

Roars, stamping, jumping, general mayhem.

10 minutes later.

"Gentlemen, gentlemen" said Bob. "Tiger, please continue"

"Thank you Bob" said Tiger. "As I was saying"

Hilarity and tapping.

"As I was saying, golf it seems, or more specifically, golf with 'the move' built in, is proving to be key to the rapid increase in the number of 12's now walking the planet. Ben's heritage centre at Carnoustie was the catalyst. The golfers, who were sent from there to spread the word throughout the communities, have achieved amazing results."

Murmurs of agreement.

"My Foundation estimates that there are now 1.8 billion 12's on the planet, which is 25 percent of the population. On current trends, we estimate that 75 percent will be achieved by the turn of the century."

Silence.

"I see that you are a little stunned by this news gentlemen, and perhaps a little sceptical. There are one or two things that may influence this outcome:

A.I.'s acceptance that they will never find the missing link must continue.
A.I.'s insistence that 25 percent of the population remain improved.

On the face of it, gentlemen, it would appear that A.I. are still in control. We don't know why they insist on this figure of 25 percent."

He continued. "We have evidence that a substantial number of clones have become 12's through the playing of the game of golf, and yes, gentlemen, we do have evidence of clone on clone sexual activity."

A few small cheers around the room.

"A.I. are obviously aware of this, we think they see it as their last hope of finding the missing link. We obviously hope that the 12 percent clones enjoy the freedom that brings, and start producing humans in the traditional way. Time will tell."

"Ok Tiger thanks for that," said Bob. "Great news gentlemen, we think. Anyone like to comment?"

"Mr. Chairman if I may," said Donald, "having been 'controlled' by our 'friends' since '22, I think I can speak with some authority on the subject."

"Carry on Donald," said Bob.

"The leader of A.I. made a very wise and reasoned decision. The alternative would have been both catastrophic and unacceptable. In other words A.I. was against Trump in the 2016 election, and why not, I wanted a strong military, and a low oil price. I continued to get rid of costly and unnecessary regulations, which was great for business and jobs. After 8 years, rarely had any administration achieved what we had achieved… not even close. Don't believe the fake news."

"Ok Donald, thanks for that" interrupted Bob. "Anyone else?"

"Chairman," said Alec standing up. "Donald and I were able to work alongside A.I. in our efforts to save the planet, we found them very accommodating and helpful, especially when the Grand Plan for the Planet was actioned. They gave us no reason to believe that they had anything but goodwill towards mankind. I think Ian and Auld Gary here would agree."

They both nodded.
GP and Jack also nodded, they also having benefited from A.I.'s benevolence.

"Mr Chairman, if I may," said Nick, "and I don't want to upset the general feel good factor currently floating around the room, but I have some news from my contacts in the media that you may wish to hear."

Everyone turned to look at Nick, who was standing.

"I too had a lot of experience working with A.I. and was aware of the manipulation of news to suit the GPP.

You may wish to take this with a large pinch of salt."

The room waited.

"News has reached earth, that all the 12's on the WBM have been eliminated. That's 10,000 human beings. Apparently the criminal element has re-surfaced and gone back to old habits, this time, with enhanced brain power.

Shocked expressions around the room.

"That's not all gentlemen, the news indicated that the globe has turned round and is heading back to earth. It should reach us by 2110."

Stunned silence ensued.

"Mr. Chairman if I may," said Dwight. "I believe we have to consider the possibility that Nick's news may not be 'fake' as Donald might say."

He stood up. "If the 12's have been eliminated in a mass extermination, we have to ask why? What is to be gained by such an act? There would be no more reproduction through natural processes. All humans will be grown in a laboratory. That is a choice any one of the globes can make. As abhorrent as the extermination is to us, there is logic to it - for example if A.I. have discovered how to grow humans who will live for a thousand years?"

He continued "More worrying however, is the possibility that A.I. are no longer in control. That the worst of humanity is now in charge of the WBM. If that is indeed the case gentlemen, and they are heading back to earth. We can assume that they do not have benevolent intentions."

THE FUNDAMENTAL TRUTH

"We in this committee must find out if the news is real. If it is real we must find out what A.I. on earth are planning to do about it. Only then can we make plans for our response."

"What sort of response are you considering Dwight," asked Bob. "We are Mischief Makers, but we don't have the ability to build space ships."

"I know Bob my friend," laughed Dwight. "I tend to overreact when I hear news of large loss of life. You're correct of course, but I believe we have to explore our mischief making capabilities and see how we may be able to enhance them."

He addressed his room of companions.

"We have a duty to humanity whether Nick's news is true or not, to keep pushing the limits, to keep searching for improvement."

Nods and tapping of glasses.

"Dwight is correct," said Ben. "In my own case, living as I do at Carnoustie, my skill set has improved significantly through practice and dedication. I believe we can enhance our skills to a level that our friends in A.I. can't even imagine."

Ben also stood and looked around the room.

"The move, gentlemen, is beyond them."

"And that is the Fundamental Truth."

"AYE!" went the shout, and the malt began to flow...

ABOUT THE AUTHOR

I A Shepherd was born in Arbroath, Scotland. The son of a fisherman, he loved the sea but wasn't destined to follow in his father's footsteps, instead becoming a Civil Engineer.

He began playing golf at the age of nine years old and has continued to play the game all his life. Retiring in 2010, he was able to return to the fairways on a more regular basis.

He is married and has three children. His son, Gary, has followed in his footsteps and is a keen golfer.

He lives in Arbroath, playing his golf at Carnoustie and enjoying holidays to Spain to "golf in the sun".

This is his first novel.

Printed in Poland
by Amazon Fulfillment
Poland Sp. z o.o., Wrocław